EMPRESS IN HIDING

EMPRESS IN HIDING

EMPRESS IN DISGUISE BOOK 2

ZOEY GONG

AMANDA ROBERTS

Red Empress Publishing
www.RedEmpressPublishing.com

Cover by Cherith Vaughan
CoversbyCherith.com

ALSO BY ZOEY GONG

Contemporary Romance

The New Year Boyfriend

The Animal Companions Series

A Girl and Her Elephant

A Girl and Her Panda

A Girl and Her Tiger

Empress in Disguise Trilogy

Empress in Disguise

Empress in Hiding

Empress in Danger

ALSO BY AMANDA ROBERTS

Fiction Novels

Threads of Silk

The Man in the Dragon Mask

Novels of the Qing Court

The Other Empress

The Pearl Concubine

The French Princess

The Qing Dynasty Mysteries

Murder in the Forbidden City

Murder in the British Quarter

Murder at the Peking Opera

The Touching Time Series

The Child's Curse

The Emperor's Seal

The Empress's Dagger

The Slave's Necklace

1

"May the empress live ten thousand years!" the sea of people before me says a second, and then a third time.

They are talking about me. *Me!* How did this happen? Only a few months ago I was living on the streets of Peking, a girl so poor I did not have a pair of shoes. A Han Chinese, not even a Manchu. And now I am the empress of China. I laugh at the absurdity of it, even though I know it is inappropriate. But I cannot help myself. I am a fraud, yet all of the most powerful men in the world—the emperor included—believe that I am their empress.

"Is there something wrong, my lady?" the emperor, my husband, Emperor Guozhi, says, laying his large hand upon my small on one the arm of my throne. I raise my eyes to the gold dragon hovering above us, the giant pearl in his mouth. I am thankful that the pearl rests over the emperor's throne and not that of the empress. There is no superstition that says that if any woman who is not the empress dares to sit on the phoenix throne, she will be crushed.

"No, your majesty," I manage to choke out. "I...It is so overwhelming. I hardly know what to think. I am sorry."

The emperor presses his lips and gives a small nod. He runs his thumb over the back of my hand, and I have the feeling that he is on the verge of tears. He loved Empress Caihong, of that I am sure. And now I am sitting in her place. No matter how much affection he has for me, he could never love me as he did her. I can never take her place —in any aspect.

"You should return to your palace," he says. "Rest. You will have many duties to attend to shortly."

My stomach is a heavy stone. How can I—an ignorant girl with no education—manage the emperor's harem of over a hundred ladies? I look to my left, to the emperor's mother, Dowager Empress Fenfang, but she is staring straight ahead, her mouth a thin line. She is the person who should help me the most. The person who should train me in my new duties. But she also despises me, I'm sure of it, just as she despised Empress Caihong before me.

I feel a tug and realize that the emperor is helping me to stand. I do so slowly. The headdress strains my neck and my legs feel wobbly inside my pot-bottom shoes. I had been laughing moments ago, but now tears fill my eyes as I look down the row of stairs I must descend. I am certain I will fall and make a fool of myself in front of the emperor, his mother, and the hundreds of gathered dignitaries. Maybe I will get lucky and I will break my neck, putting an end to this ridiculous farce.

But I raise my eyes and they fall on Prince Honghui. Our gaze meets, and it gives me strength. He believes in me. He thinks I can do this. I think he is wrong, but I at least have to try. I have lost him, we can never be lovers again, never kiss, never hold hands, never speak privately, but I can still be the woman he thinks I am—even if that woman doesn't exist.

My maids, Nuwa and Suyin, each take one of my hands. I hold onto them tightly, as I have always relied on them ever since I first entered the Forbidden City. They descend the stairs ahead of me by one step, and I lean into them heavily, the headdress threatening to send me crashing to the floor below.

But I do not fall, not with my steady servants by my side. When I am safely at the foot of the dais, I raise my head and look over the sea of kowtowing bodies. Even the prince is bent over so that I cannot see his face, but I know he's there. He will always be there.

My maids walk beside me as I leave the audience hall. Outside, in the bright sunshine, my chief eunuch, Jinhai, is waiting for me. His neck is bent, but I can still see the pleased smile on his face. He helps me into my sedan chair, closing the flaps around me. He is right to be happy, him and all my servants. They have not served in the Forbidden City very long, but all of them—like me, their lady—have climbed as high as is possible. With the income they now earn, they will never want for anything, and they will be able to support their families as well. Suyin, when the time comes, will be able to make a good marriage, perhaps even to a palace official.

I suddenly realize how many people are now dependent on me. I am young, and the emperor is not old. I could retain my position for decades. Thus, my servants could remain with me, building their own savings or supporting their families for all that time as well. But if I were to die, be it by tripping in my ridiculous shoes or in childbirth, their comfortable lives would be at an end. They would be dismissed or reassigned to a woman of lower station. Dying would put an end to my misery, to the lies that hold me captive, and I have prayed for it many times. But that would be selfish. I must live, and I must do my best to remain in the emperor's good graces, if not for myself, then for those around me. I owe it to them. I never would have attained my current position without them. I did not want it, but now that I have it, I cannot throw it away. This is my life now, and I must accept it.

When my sedan chair stops moving and I am helped out, I am surprised to see that we are not in front of my palace, the Palace of Earthly Honors, but Empress Caihong's palace. The place where she lived—and the place where she died. I lose my breath for a moment at the memory of holding her in my arms as the life slipped from her. The vision of her bleeding body after her son had been cut from her belly makes me shudder. I lose my footing, stepping backward, but thankfully, my maids are there to keep me from falling.

"My lady," Suyin says, "are you all right?"

I look around and see a dozen eunuch servants shuffling about, carrying items from my palace into this one.

"What is happening?" I ask. "Why are they moving my things?"

"You are the empress now," Jinhai says. "You are to live in the empress's palace."

"No!" I say with more force than I intended, but I am horrified at the thought. "No, I will not live here. Take me back home, back to the Palace of Earthly Honors, now!"

I see that the eunuchs have slowed their work, looking at me, but they do not stop. From inside the palace, Fiyanggu, the chief eunuch for domestic affairs, comes out. He orders the other eunuch servants around and then he kneels before me.

"Your majesty," he says, "I am sorry the move is not yet complete. All will be set right shortly, I assure you."

"No!" I say again. "Stop this. Stop it now!"

Fiyanggu gets to his feet but keeps his face downcast. "Stop what, your majesty?"

"Stop moving things! I will not live here. Take my things back home now."

"I-I-It is tradition for the empress to reside here, in the Palace of—"

"I don't care," I say. "I will not live in this place, where the floors are stained with blood."

"I assure you, my lady, that everything has been cleaned to exacting standards—"

"I don't care!" I say again, trying to stomp my foot but finding it impossible to do so. "I will always remember what happened here. It is not a palace, it is a tomb. I'll not live here." I'm near to tears and am on the verge of throwing a fit.

Fiyanggu hesitates, and I see that all the other eunuchs have stopped to watch me, but still no one obeys me. I feel Suyin lean very close to me.

"You are the empress," she whispers in my ear so quietly, I barely hear her.

"I know!" I say, exasperated. But when I look at her, I realize that she is not saying that, as empress, I must live here. She is telling me to use my position to my advantage. I clear my throat and stand up straight, summoning my dignity to give me a strength I do not feel.

"I am the empress," I say, my voice even while my body shakes. "And you will do as I say. Remove my things from this place and put them back in the Palace of Earthly Honors."

"The-the-the emperor—" Fiyanggu tries, but I cut him off.

"Is not the head of the inner court," I say. "I am. Do as I command."

Fiyanggu kowtows again before backing away from me and barking orders at the eunuchs. At once, they begin moving the many items back in the direction of my palace. I breathe a sigh of relief and am on the verge of collapse.

"You did excellent, my lady," Suyin says as she and Nuwa help me back into the sedan chair.

"I only hope the emperor is not angry with me," I say. Fiyanggu was only acting under his orders, after all.

"He was only following protocol, I'm sure," Jinhai says. "Fiyanggu was correct in saying that it is tradition for the empress to live here. But as the empress, you may live wherever you please. You could even take one of the other ladies' palaces if you wished."

"I will not turn anyone out of her home," I say. "I only wish to not live in a palace with such haunting memories."

"Of course," he says with a bow.

Only a few moments later, I am standing in front of the Palace of Earthly Honors, and I let out a sigh. In all the changes that have occurred recently, at least where I will lay my head tonight remains the same.

In my dressing room, the phoenix crown placed upon my head by the empress dowager is removed first and set upon a pillow on a pedestal. The crown is only worn for ceremonial events, but it is always to be treated with honor. After that, the headdress is removed, as is the heavy robe, and the pot-bottom shoes are taken from my feet. It is a relief to have such weights removed from my body, even if my soul is still heavy.

How am I going to do this? How can I be empress? I

don't even know what all the position entails. I was not one of the empress's ladies. I didn't see what her life was like most of the day. I only saw her in the mornings for greetings. I need help. I have my servants, of course, but I need more than that. I then remember my friends, Yanmei and Wangli. I have barely seen them since I was first elevated. I do not know if they retreated from me out of jealousy or something else, but I did not want to force my company upon them if they did not want it. But now that I am the empress, they will not be able to refuse my invitations.

"Suyin, let Lady Yanmei and Lady Wangli know that I wish to take tea with them."

"Of course, my lady," Suyin says, and then she is gone.

"How much of an impression do you want to make on them, my lady?" Nuwa asks, and I chuckle. I know she means, how ornate do I wish my appearance to be?

"None at all," I say. "I hope to earn their friendship back, not punish them for their past slights against me."

"Of course." Nuwa styles my hair simply, wipes away most of my makeup, and dresses me in a subdued, dark blue robe and shoes with the smallest pot-bottom at my disposal. When I hear a commotion outside, I am surprised at how quickly they have arrived. I rush to the courtyard, eager to see my friends.

But it is not my friends who come through the gate into my garden.

"Dowager Empress Fenfeng!" a eunuch announces as the older woman appears.

I completely forget myself and my new position, falling to my knees and kneeling before her. I hear her sigh and click her tongue.

"What a disappointment you are," she says.

Sadly, I cannot disagree.

2

——————

"Get up," Fenfeng commands me. I do as she says, but I keep my eyes downcast. "Never fall to your knees before me again. Do you understand?"

"Yes, Mother," I say. As the emperor's mother and my mother-in-law, custom dictate that I refer to her as "Mother," so I do so. It always turns my stomach, though. How I miss my own mother! If only I could reach out to her, tell her what has become of me. But that would be far too dangerous. If anyone ever knew that I was not really Lihua, the penalty would be death for treason.

"Are you listening to me?" Fenfeng asks.

"Yes, Mother," I say even though I have not heard a word she's said. There is so much going on around me, I can hardly focus.

"You are the empress, now," she says, shaking her head as though she cannot believe it. "You will now be in charge of managing the harem. I will be watching you, Lihua. Do not disappoint me." She turns to leave.

"Wait," I say, following her. "Won't you help me? I don't know how to be an empress. Can you teach me?"

She turns back to me slowly, and I am sure I see a hint of a smile on her face that she quickly hides as she faces me. "In the past, when I have attempted to guide you, you have resisted my efforts."

This is only partly true. I have always done as Fenfeng has asked of me, except in one area: the emperor's children. The emperor has two daughters, one by the late empress, and one by Lady An, who is also now dead. I feel great empathy for these children who have no mother and rarely see their father. I suppose I feel a kinship with them since I no longer have my parents either. I adore the girls and want nothing more than to protect them. But for some reason, Dowager Empress Fenfeng does not like me meddling in her efforts to raise the girls. I'm not sure what to say. I need the empress's help, but I do not want her to take the children from me.

"A thousand apologies, Mother," I say. "I know that you are far wiser than myself in all things. I would be honored if you would help me."

She presses her lips. It is not the answer she wants, but neither is it one she can reject.

"Very well," she says, her voice tight. "I will do my best to help you. Spend today getting your house in order. After audiences tomorrow, I will give you more directions."

"Thank you, Mother," I say, bending my knees and neck in a polite bow. It is a great relief when she is gone.

"You know that she has no desire to teach you anything," Suyin whispers to me. "She only wishes to control you. To regain her position as head of the harem."

"I know," I say, going to a stone table and sitting on one of the matching stone stools. "But I do need her help. I have no idea what I am doing. And while you and Nuwa and Jinhai have been very helpful in teaching me the ways of the Forbidden City, it's not enough. Only Fenfeng knows what it is like to be an empress."

Suyin lets out a sigh. "I only hope you know what you are doing."

Of course I don't, I want to say, but I hold my tongue. I am at a complete loss for what to do next. It is fine and easy for the emperor to name me empress. But how to fill that role is something he cannot teach me.

I hear voices and footsteps and see Yanmei and Wangli step into the garden. I nearly jump to my feet as I rush over to greet them. They drop down to their knees before me.

"Greetings, empress," they say.

"Please stand," I say, touching them lightly on the shoulders. They do, but they keep their eyes downcast, not looking at me. I step closer to them and speak in a low voice. "Please, I need my friends. I am so lost! Do not treat me like a stranger."

Yanmei and Wangli look at each other and seem to have a conversation with their eyes that I am not privy to.

"Very well," Yanmei says, and a cautious smile crosses her face. "It is good to see you, my lady."

I take her hands in mine. "Call me Lihua when we are in private, I beg you." It is not my name, but at least it is less formal than "empress" or "lady."

"I am surprised you did not change your name," Wangli says as we all walk back to the table and sit while maids bring tea and sweet and savory treats.

"What?" I ask.

"You know, it is tradition for a person to take a new name when elevated to a higher position," she explains.

I blink dumbly. This must be a Manchu tradition. One I had no way of knowing since no one asked if I wished to change my name before the ceremony. I wish I had known!

I would have changed my name from Lihua back to Daiyu. How I long to hear someone use my real name!

"I...I was so overwhelmed with everything, I didn't think of it," I say.

"No matter," Yanmei says. "Lihua is a beautiful name."

I hate the name Lihua, but I smile and nod. I hate that Lihua—the real Lihua—stole my life from me. She and her mother, Mingxia, lied to me to get me to take Lihua's place at the consort selection. They said I wouldn't be chosen. That I would certainly fail the examination process. But that is not what happened at all. They knew that Lihua would advance to the final round easily since she has a birth date that is auspicious when compared to the emperor's birth chart. Still, the fact that I was chosen in the end was by mere chance. My name drawn from a bowl. But the chance that I would be selected was much higher than I was led to believe. While I thought that I would quickly fail the examination and then be allowed to return home, Mingxia knew with a fair amount of certainty that when I entered the Forbidden City, I would never leave.

I try to push my anger and resentment aside—at least for now. There is nothing I can do about it. I must keep my true identity a secret. But one day I hope I will have the opportunity to confront Mingxia and Lihua for their lies.

"I have a gift for each of you," I tell Yanmei and Wangli, trying to turn my thoughts to happier subjects. "I have decided to elevate you both to rank-three consorts." They gasp and look at me, then each other, and then back to me again.

"Why?" Yanmei asks.

"Can you do that?" Wangli asks.

"I believe it is in my authority," I say. "I would like each of you to serve as my ladies-in-waiting, so you deserve higher ranks."

"But...rank three?" Yanmei asks. "Is that not reserved for the mothers of Emperor Guozhi's children?"

"Well, as rank-three consorts, perhaps you will both become mothers soon," I say. "A higher rank means that you will be called to his bed more often."

"What a blessing that would be!" Yanmei says, but Wangli's reaction is a bit more reserved.

"This is very kind of you," she says. "Especially.... Well, especially considering how Yanmei and I have treated you ever since you were elevated."

I reach out and take Wangli's hand. "It is forgotten, I promise you. This has been a strange time for all of us. I did not reach out to you as much as I should have either. But now that I am empress, I cannot do this alone. I need help from my friends."

"I am not sure how much help we will be to you," Yanmei says, filling our teacups with fresh, hot tea. "We don't know anything about being empress."

"You might have a large palace, countless servants, and chests of gold," Wangli says, "but I would not want to be in your position."

"Oh?" I ask. This surprises me. Of course, the first time I met Wangli, she was crying in the garden. She told me then that she didn't want to be here. But I had assumed that her views on the matter had changed. After all, don't all Manchu girls dream of one day becoming empress? Of bearing the emperor a son and being the mother of the next emperor? If she wasn't jealous of me, why did she turn so cold after I was elevated?

She nibbles in a sweet, steamed bun for a moment

before speaking. "The way the other ladies talk about you..." She shakes her head. "It is not kind."

I nod. "I expected as much," I say. As I said, most Manchu girls dream of being empress. Since I am in that role, and very young, the other ladies will never have that chance—unless I die. The thought sours my stomach and I put down the fried, spicy tofu I had been eating. My biggest fear had been dying in childbirth, like Empress Caihong. But a new worry settles over me. What if I am murdered? What if someone tries to poison me or sends an assassin? Caihong was well-liked and respected by the other harem ladies, but someone still sent an assassin to kill her. He was unsuccessful, thank Heaven, but I do not believe Lady An was behind the plot. The real killer is still out there. And what if she comes for me next?

"The ladies would be jealous no matter who the empress was," Yanmei says. "You surely heard the cruel talk about Caihong before she died."

I shake my head. "Other than the two of you, I have not had any friends, so I was not familiar with much gossip. I can hardly imagine what they must think of me. Caihong was a princess, so beautiful and elegant. And she was so kind! I can never live up to her."

"And you shouldn't try to," Wangli says. "You are not Caihong. You are Lihua. You will be a wonderful empress. It will just take time for you to figure out what you are doing."

"We saw Dowager Empress Fenfeng leaving as we arrived," Yanmei says. "She will surely help you."

"Yes," I say. "That is why she was here, or at least why she said she was here. She said she is willing to guide me, but I think she wants to control me." The girls nod thoughtfully.

"I can see why she would want to be in charge of the

harem," Yanmei says. "What else is she going to do with herself? Being a dowager, with her children grown and a new empress in her place, must be a terribly boring life. But, surely she would want you to succeed. Does she not want the emperor to finally have a son?"

"She wants to keep Guozhi's children from me," I say. "I'm not exactly sure why. If I have a son, do you suppose she will want to take him from me as well?"

"She might," Wangli says. "She could control the throne itself if she controlled the emperor's heir."

I have a feeling we are wading into dangerous territory with such talk, and my palace is full of servants I do not yet know. I cannot risk my words getting back to the dowager.

"Well, I need her help—for now. I will have to do as she tells me."

Yanmei and Wangli nod and sip their tea while we sit in awkward silence for a moment.

"You will both be moved to larger palaces," I say. "As befitting your station."

"It will be so nice not to have to share space with other ladies," Yanmei says.

"And you will have more servants and larger allowances."

"My family will certainly be glad of that," Wangli says.

"As will mine," Yanmei adds in.

"Good," I say, standing. "Well, I will need to inform Fiyanggu about your promotions. I should let you return home to prepare for moving."

They both stand and then kneel before me. I hate it, but I cannot stop them. They cannot appear above the rules in front of others.

"We will see you at morning audiences," Wangli says as I walk them to the gate.

"I will talk to Suyin and find out what duties a lady-in-waiting will actually have," I say. "I don't really know. I just want to have you both close to me."

We all hug and kiss goodbye. As I watch them leave, my heart feels a little lighter. At least I won't be going through this completely alone.

3

———

Hosting my first morning greeting as empress goes smoothly, but I keep it very short. After everyone kneels and waves their handkerchiefs at me and then Dowager Empress Fenfeng, I announce that Yanmei and Wangli have been promoted. I then single out Lady Euhmeh, one of the girls I shared a palace with when I first arrived at the Forbidden City.

"You helped Lady An and Empress Caihong manage the harem, including the accounts, correct?" I say.

"Yes, my lady," she responds, looking at the floor.

"I hope you will do the same for me. Please, call on me this afternoon and we can discuss your new duties."

"Yes, my lady," she says with a small bow before sinking back into her seat.

"That is all. Dismissed." I let out a sigh of relief as the women all file out of the room.

"Did I do well, Mother?" I ask Fenfeng. I don't really care what she thinks, but I believe she will feel flattered if she thinks that I do care.

Fenfeng sits up a little straighter and I see a smirk

quickly cross her face. "I suppose. Send for me when Lady Euhmeh arrives at your palace. I should be there to discuss her duties. And make sure your ladies-in-waiting are there as well."

"I will, Mother. Thank you."

She nods and is then escorted out of the audience hall by her ladies and eunuchs. Suyin helps me stand, but as I walk to the door, I hear a voice behind me.

"Empress?"

I turn around and see Lady Chunhua kneeling. I don't know her, other than the fact that we were selected at random to be consorts at the same time. There are several other ladies with her, but I do not yet know their names.

"Yes?" I ask. Chunhua stands, but keeps her eyes down.

"I wanted to tell you that I think you will make an excellent empress."

"Really?" I ask. None of the other girls have reached out to me before, even those I used to share a house with. No one has ever said as much as a kind word to me. Though, that was how I preferred it. I did not reach out to anyone because I was afraid that if I got too close to anyone, my secrets might be discovered.

Chunhua looks at me directly and takes my hand in hers. "Of course! I knew it the moment you gave a birthday gift to the emperor's brother that you were a kind and thoughtful person."

"Thank you," I say, feeling a little more at ease. "I thought... Well, I was afraid that everyone hated me."

The gathered girls all stand and gather around me, releasing a chorus of reassurance.

"Of course not!"

"We think you are wonderful."

"Such a good empress."

I have to take a step back to keep from being crushed. "Umm... Thank you. Would you all like to come over for tea?"

The girls all screech in excitement and clap their hands. Then they gather around me again to express their thanks.

"Okay," I say. "Let's go, then. I'm already hungry."

"Are you pregnant already?" one lady asks.

"Oh! Is the empress pregnant?" another asks.

"Congratulations!" another says.

"No!" I try to say quickly, but not before the rumor spreads through the little crowd. "No, I'm not pregnant. At least, I don't think so."

"I'm sure you will be soon."

"You are so lucky to get to spend so many nights with the emperor."

The girls chatter all around me, so much so that I can hardly follow the conversations. When we arrive at the palace, though, they immediately scatter. They explore the gardens, the kitchen, and I see a few try to enter my bedroom, but a maid stops them and guards the door.

I'm a bit disappointed. I thought that they all—or at least some of them—wanted to be my friends. But it seems that they only wanted to see how an empress lives. I can't fault them for being curious, though, so I say nothing. Nuwa goes to the kitchen to tell the cook to prepare tea for the large crowd. I motion Yanmei and Wangli to me.

"I'm starting to think that inviting them all here was a mistake."

"Starting to?" Wangli says, raising an eyebrow. "They don't want to be your friend. They only want whatever they think they can get from you."

"You promoted us to rank-three consorts," Yanmei says. "They are all certain to be looking for similar favors."

"Empress?"

I turn around and see one of the "guests," but I don't know her name. She is a small, thin girl with a sweet face. I would swear the girl is too young to be of child-bearing age if I didn't know better. She must have been chosen during the same selection process that I was, but I don't remember her.

"Yes?"

"I brought these for you." She holds out a basket of small oranges. "They grow outside my palace and I thought you would enjoy them."

"Thank you," I say as I accept the basket. I, of course, have no shortage of whatever fruits I want. But to be given fruit as a gift... Well, that's never happened before, so I am quite touched. I hand the basket to Suyin.

"Have these included among the snacks the cook is preparing."

"Yes, my lady."

"What is your name?" I ask the girl.

"Shulan, my lady," she says with a bow.

"It's a pleasure to meet you." I hear splashing and look over to see that some ladies are sitting with their feet in my pond. I grimace at that. Of course, on a hot day, putting my feet in the pond is quite refreshing. But I would not be so brazen as to put my feet into the empress's pond without permission! And the way they are splashing around, I'm sure they will frighten my fish. I want to tell them to stop, but I don't want to appear rude or cruel. I want all of the ladies to like me if possible, so I don't say anything for now. But later, I will let the maids know that they should stop any girls who attempt to take such liberties.

As my eyes rove around the courtyard, I see one young

woman staring at a painting on one of the walls, one that I painted. I walk over and ask her what she thinks of it.

"Did you paint this?" she asks.

"Yes."

"Then I suppose I should say that it is wonderful."

I chuckle. "And if I didn't paint it?"

"In that case, it's rather terrible." I'm shocked at her candor, but then she looks at me with a wide smile and we burst out laughing.

"I am only teasing you," she says. "It's not good. But you do have some talent. If you keep practicing, I'm sure you will improve quickly."

"I only practice painting when my eyes or fingers are too tired from embroidery," I say. "That is where my true talent lies. My mother taught me, and she was quite skilled."

This girl looks older than me by some years. I think she looks to be about the deceased empress's age, so I think she must have been here for some time. She was probably one of the first concubines selected for Guozhi.

"Forgive me," I say. "But I have not learned everyone's names. Who are you?"

"Huiyin, my lady," she says with a bow.

"And I suppose you know a lot about painting, considering your strong opinions on the matter."

"I enjoy it, certainly," she says. "My father was a calligrapher, so he taught me to write and paint."

"That's wonderful," I say. "Perhaps you and I could paint together and you could help me."

Her face brightens. "I would enjoy that, my lady."

I see the cook and several of her helpers bring trays of tea and snacks into the courtyard, placing them on the several small tables scattered about. There is no single table large enough for everyone. The girls all look at the snacks appreciatively, but no one takes a seat. I realize they are all waiting for me.

I go to the center table and sit down. The other girls all rush to the other seats, pushing each other aside in hopes of snagging a place. One girl cries out in pain when she topples off her shoes and hits the ground. I jump back to my feet.

"Stop this!" I yell, more forcefully than I intended. Everyone goes silent and then drops to their knees. They all begin uttering a hundred apologies.

"No, please don't do that," I say, but I am not sure they can hear me over their blubbering. I look helplessly to Suyin, who mimes clapping her hands together. I nod and then clap my hands loud enough to be heard.

"Stop this!" I say again, and this time the girls go quiet. "My ladies-in-waiting shall sit with me. As will..." I look around at the expectant faces, but I have no idea who to choose, so I just say the few names I have learned today. "Chunhua, Huiyin, and Shulan."

The five lucky chosen ones step from the crowd and take their seats at the table. I follow suit, and the remaining ladies all sigh in disappointment as they find seats elsewhere.

"That was rather a mess," I say, more to myself than anyone else, but Shulan responds.

"They only want the chance to be near you," she says.

"They can't all be near her at the same time," Wangli grumbles.

I nod. "Yes, I should have planned better, I suppose. I shouldn't have invited everyone at once. I was just so surprised that anyone wanted to be near me at all."

"You are the empress," Yanmei says. "Whether they like

you or not, they are going to want to be near you for all the gifts you can bestow on them."

I stare at her for a moment. "Gifts? Am I supposed to give everyone a gift?"

"Well, not necessarily to everyone right now," Chunhua says, her words careful. "But just as you reward your servants, you should also reward your ladies. But you can do much more for everyone than give them gifts."

"What else can I give them?" I ask.

"Time with the emperor, of course," Chunhua says, and I blush. I know that Guozhi sleeps with all the women of the harem, but it is not something I like to dwell on, and certainly not talk about openly.

"I don't have anything to do with that," I say. "His eunuchs and the domestic affairs office schedules such matters."

"But you can encourage him to select certain women too," Huiyin says. "It is one of your duties, actually."

I look at her, confused. I was not aware of this, nor is it something I want to do.

"As the head of the harem, you know the ladies best. And as empress, you know his majesty best. As such, you are in the best position to know which of us the emperor might find most...pleasing."

Her words make sense, but they still give me unease. I think back to the one time I did try to influence his majesty to show favor to someone else. Lady An. As the mother of his first daughter, I thought she would stand a good chance of giving the emperor a son. I also knew how despondent she was and wished to help her.

But my meddling backfired. The emperor despised Lady An and we had a terrible fight over the matter. I shake my head. That is something I certainly do not wish to repeat.

"I don't know..." I say. "I...I...I suppose I should get to know all the ladies better first. I cannot make any recommendations until I learn more about each of them." The ladies all nod in agreement.

"You are very wise, my lady," Shulan says, looking at me adoringly. I blush.

"Hardly," I say. "I'm quite stupid. I'm not nearly as educated or cultured as most of the ladies in the harem."

"That is not true," Wangli says. "You would not be where you are today if you were stupid."

"You knew to give the prince a gift," Shulan says.

"You saved Empress Caihong's life," Chunhua says.

"I heard that you saved her twice," Yanmei says. "First when you alerted the guards to the assassin, and then again when she thought she was having a miscarriage. You kept her calm and knew what to do to save the baby...at least at the time."

My eyes water at the memory. I had been honored to save Caihong's life. She had been a kind woman and a good empress. It is so unfair that she died. And such a horrible death at that.

"I just feel as if everything that has happened to me has been pure chance," I say. "My name was selected randomly from a bowl. It could have been anyone else."

"But it wasn't anyone else," Huiyin says. "It was you. Heaven willed it, don't you see? You were meant to be here."

I look around the table at all the smiling faces agreeing with her. I'm the only one who thinks—knows—she's wrong. I lied to get here. Took Lihua's place. Pretend every day to be someone and something I'm not. I have wondered many times if Heaven has a plan for me. If I am meant to be here. It would be a comforting thought, but I simply can't believe it. Eventually, I will be discovered. I'm sure of it.

But I can't tell anyone any of this. I can only smile and nod and agree. "Thank you," I say.

Finally, one by one, the ladies take their leave—and a few teacups, chopsticks, and extra snacks as well. I don't stop them, though. What is a teacup or extra steamed bun to me? I have far more of everything than I could ever need. And if I were to catch any of the girls stealing, I'd have to punish them. I'd rather them rob me blind than have to do that.

But when I am alone again, I feel a sense of emptiness. I miss my family. No one here really knows me, and I will have to always be careful about what I say or do. I wish I could reach out to my parents and sisters. Just make sure they are okay. Let them know that I am safe...relatively. I am at least safe for the moment. The empress of China, favored by the emperor. Of course, I could lose all of it in a moment.

I remember how I was once so desperate to see my family that I dared to climb over the red walls of the Forbidden City. That had been stupid, dangerous. If I could go back and tell myself not to do it, I would. And yet the pull to see my family, to try and find them, is so strong, I might be heading for a similar mistake. I have no plan for how I might be able to reach out to them, but if the opportunity were to present itself, I would not hesitate to take it.

4

It is the first night that the emperor has sent for me since I was crowned empress. I'm surprisingly nervous! I pace the room as I wait for the sedan chair to arrive. I have been in the emperor's bed more times than I can count, but we have not been together for weeks. We fought, and then Caihong died. The emperor has not even visited my palace during the day since I became empress. I have tried not to let it bother me. He is a busy man, and I have had plenty to focus on, so I am hardly bored or lonely.

Still, in the back of my mind, it seems strange. Has he forgotten me? Is he still angry with me? Did he only name me empress because tradition dictated it even if he did not want to?

I am sure I am worrying needlessly. I am heartened by the fact that the emperor has not called any woman to his bed since Caihong died. No one else has taken my place in his heart or his bed, it seems.

Now that I am empress, I no longer have to be taken to the emperor naked, but am carried in my nightclothes by sedan chair. It is far more dignified, and if I could change the rules to allow the other women to be carried in such a manner when they are summoned by the emperor, then I would do it. But change is a difficult thing, and I will need to choose my battles wisely.

I sit on the emperor's bed, twirling my long hair between my fingers as I wait for him to appear. Several times, I hear voices or a door open and close, but the emperor does not appear. He has never kept me waiting before. He is usually in the room, already in the bed, when he sends for me. It seems as though everything has changed since I became empress, even the smallest things.

Finally, the door to the bed-chamber opens and the emperor breezes in. I jump to my feet, and then I kneel. He holds his hand out to me, and I take it as he helps me stand.

"Lihua," he says, "how good it is to see you."

I smile up at him and cannot help but notice that his face has changed since I saw him last. There are wrinkles around his eyes and dark circles under them. His skin is dry, as if he has not been taking care of himself as he should. But the most apparent change is the heavy sadness that hangs on his every feature like a cloud. I suppose I let my concern show on my own face because he turns away from me.

"Leave us!" he orders his eunuchs. "Are you not happy to see me?"

"Of course I am!" I say. "I have missed you terribly."

"Then why is your face so grave?"

"I could ask you the same thing," I say, "but I already know the answer."

He opens his mouth to say something, as if to protest, but he then closes it and shakes his head. He sits on the bed with a long exhale. I sit lightly beside him.

"You loved her, didn't you?" I say after a moment. "She

was not merely the woman you had been ordered to marry, was she? She was much more than that."

He leans forward on his knees. "Do you know how she came to be empress?"

I shake my head, but he's not looking at me, so I say, "No. I only know that she was a princess, so I had once thought it was a political marriage. But after seeing the two of you together, and the way you grieve, I know she was more to you than that."

"Our relationship with the Mongolians has been stable for some time," he says. "We may squabble over borders or trade occasionally, but we are allies.

"I accompanied my father on a routine visit to the region. He was teaching me all there was to know about being emperor, and maintaining our friendship with Mongolia was part of it. That was the first time I saw her, sitting by her father's side as he welcomed us into his yurt.

"She was exquisite. She wore a hat edged with fur and large, turquoise earrings. Her clothes were yellow and heavily beaded down the front. She looked down her long nose at me as we were introduced...and I was utterly captivated by her.

"Over the next week, I took every opportunity to see her. She loved to ride her horse, so every day, I would accompany her on long rides over the steppes at the foot of these great, white mountains."

I marvel at this. I have never seen a Manchu or Han woman ride a horse. I would never have imagined Caihong riding along the plains, her hair—still long—waving in the breeze.

"What a sight she must have been," I say breathlessly.

Guozhi nods. "She was. So, when it was time for me to marry, I wanted no one else in the world but her. But her father was not in favor of the match. He wanted her to marry a Mongolian lord. I could understand that since Manchu emperors usually only marry Manchu women. But I had to have her. So, every time his price for her went up in an attempt to dissuade me, I agreed to it." He laughs. "If it had been up to her father, we would still be squabbling over her price today. But eventually the number grew high enough that his lords and advisors pressured him to accept the terms."

"That's why her bride price was so high," I say.

"Oh? What do you know about it?" he asks me.

"Only that it was a lot of money," I say. "Some of the other ladies told me as much, but that was all. It was never shared why it was so high. I just assumed that as a princess, her price was naturally more than most."

"That was a very small part of it," he says. "But I believed she was worth it. Spread out over a life together of fifty years or so, the money would not seem like much. That is how long I thought we would be together. A lifetime."

He goes quiet again. *A lifetime.* Fifty years. I am now only eighteen years old, and to me, fifty years is beyond my reckoning. Is there even anyone in the palace who is fifty years old? Much less nearing seventy? Nuwa seems old to me and she is only in her thirties.

"The worst part," Guozhi says, breaking into my thoughts, "is that had she never gotten pregnant, she would still be alive today."

"You can't dwell on that," I say. "She wanted to give you a son. It was her duty; she told me as much."

Guozhi stands and paces. "I know that childbirth has an element of risk for a woman. That the chance of death is high. But...but I never thought it would happen to her. Was she not the daughter of Heaven? I was prideful, foolish. I should have put her safety first."

"What do you mean?" I ask. "The only way you could have kept her from falling pregnant would be to...to not summon her to your bed."

"If I had known that she was going to die, it would have been a small price to pay. That she died and our son with her, her death was meaningless."

I have to wonder at this. For a moment, I think about Honghui, the emperor's brother. The man I foolishly fell in love with and took as a lover for a short time. If we could marry, would I give up the physical joy of lovemaking in order to not fall pregnant? I'm not sure I would. Even after my mother's miscarriage, she eventually fell pregnant again, and I know my father loved her. Love and desire go hand in hand, I think.

"You can't think that way," I say. "It's not your fault."

"But it is," he says, his voice rough. "I should have put my empress ahead of my vanity. I have a hundred other women to give me children. But my empress—" He shakes his head. "—she was more precious to me than all of them put together."

All of them. That includes me. Just one of a hundred concubines waiting at the emperor's pleasure. I meant nothing more to him than any other woman. For some reason, the knowledge hurts. Or maybe it is only him saying the words out loud that hurts. He is not saying anything that isn't true. But still...for some reason, I thought I was different.

"That is why I have not called you back to my bed before now," he says, and the breath flies out of me.

"What?" I somehow manage to ask.

He sits down on the bed next to me again and takes my hands. "I do not want to lose another empress. I *will* not."

"What are you saying?" I ask, my emotions in turmoil. I never wanted this. Never wanted to be empress. Never wanted to be called to the emperor's bed at all. But now that I am here, now that I *am* empress, I feel gravely insulted that he would not want me as a proper wife.

"I...*care* deeply for you, Lihua," he says, petting my hair down the side of my face. "You have been a great comfort to me, a fine companion. And a pleasurable lover. It is my honor to have made you my empress. But I'll not lose you as I lost Caihong."

Tears run down my cheeks. "Am I never to know you as a wife again? Am I never to be a mother?"

"All of my children will be your children. That is your reward as my empress."

"It's not the same," I say, trying to explain but not finding the words.

"Is it not better to know that you will live?" he asks me.

"No!" I tell him. "It is a risk I was born to take. It is my right as a woman to have children of my own." I have never been particularly passionate about the idea of having children. I always just assumed that they would come when it was time and I would love them. That is the way of things. But to be told that I will never be *allowed* to have children? I'm horrified. Disgusted even. "How dare you take this from me?"

He looks shocked, but the more I think about it, the more incensed I become. I gave up everything to be here. I have no idea what has become of my family, and I probably will never know. I am alone in the world. If I had a child, at least I would have a family again that was all my own. I love the emperor's other children, of course. Jiangfei and

Dongmei are very precious to me. But they are not my children.

"I-I-I thought you would be pleased to know that I care so much for you," he stammers. "I only want to keep you safe. I can't bear the thought of losing you."

"I'll not be a bird in a cage," I say. We stare at each other for a moment. My breath is hot and angry as it pours through my nostrils.

"Lihua..." he whispers.

I rush to him and press my lips to his. I remove my robe so that I am naked before him. Then I untie his sash and open his robe so that our bodies are pressed together. He takes my face in his hands and kisses me eagerly. Hungrily. He is already aroused. I push him back on the bed and straddle him as I take my pleasure.

I know it pleases him too.

5

"The emperor is coming here for dinner?" I ask.

"Yes, your majesty," Fiyanggu tells me.

"Why?"

Fiyanggu chuckles. "The emperor usually eats the evening meal with one of his ladies. He used to eat with Empress Caihong most often, but this will be the first time he has eaten outside of his own room since her death."

I was aware that the emperor often had dinner with Caihong, but I never thought much of it. He never ate with me, so I thought that such an honor was reserved for the empress... I close my eyes tight for a moment as I remember that *I* am now empress. All the rights and privileges that only Caihong once enjoyed are now *my* rights and privileges.

Fiyanggu retreats with a bow as I sink onto a stool and my servants surround me.

"I don't think I'll ever get used to being treated like an empress," I say.

Suyin giggles. "But you are the empress, my lady."

"Am I?" I ask, shaking my head. "I suppose I am in name. But it feels... It feels as though the position is not really mine. That I am only holding it for a short time for someone else."

"Who?" Suyin asks. "You cannot think that the emperor will replace you?"

"He could, of course," I say. "But that is not what I mean. I don't know. I suppose I feel as though Caihong is still the empress. That she was, and still is, the real empress. I am only playacting."

"You know that isn't true," Suyin says. "Caihong was the *first* empress. You are empress now."

I shrug. Of course, I am not a real empress. I'm not who I claim to be at all. I could be discovered at any moment and... I shudder to think of what will happen to me if—when—that happens. Even now, my heart will not allow me to feel safe.

～

As Emperor Guozhi enters the courtyard, I and all my servants crouch before him in a bow.

"Welcome to my palace, your majesty," I say. The emperor offers me his hand and pulls me to my feet.

"It is a pleasure to be here this evening," he says. "I'm famished."

I lead him into one of the many sitting rooms that has been set up for eating. There are only two seats at the large, round table, which quickly is covered with over a dozen dishes for us to choose from.

"I was so surprised when I heard that you wanted to eat with me this evening," I say. I try to make conversation to cover the fact that I can hardly eat. My hands are shaking so badly, I don't think I could get even a grain of rice into my mouth without dropping it. Not to mention how tight my stomach feels.

"I am sorry I did not come sooner," he says, his voice a little sad. "I needed time."

"I understand," I say. "I'm sure I am not even half the company that Caihong was."

He looks at me curiously before putting down his bowl and chopsticks and wiping his mouth. "Why do you always speak of yourself in such low terms? Humility is a charming trait in a woman. But you seem to think you have no worth at all."

It is because I have no worth, I think. In my old life—my real life—I did not even have a single coin for a dowry. Only one of my many gowns is worth more money than I would have seen in a lifetime living in the hutongs. I cannot say any of this, of course, so I push the words and feelings into a deeply hidden part of my heart. He looks at me expectantly, though, so I must say something.

"I am here quite by accident," I say. "You drew my name from a bowl. I was not chosen on merit, and neither because you desired me. I feel as though any other concubine in the Forbidden City would be a more capable empress than myself."

He gives a small chuckle, but there is no humor in it. "I have wondered, many times, how you, the last girl selected, one who's name I drew from a bowl, became my empress."

I blink in surprise. He has had the same doubts I have? I never thought about him giving much consideration to those of us in the harem. We live in two separate worlds, worlds that only cross paths in the emperor's bed-chamber.

"But then I think of how you came to have that position," he goes on. "Your kindness. Your thoughtfulness. Your bravery. I believe you are meant to be here. It may appear that you were only chosen as a concubine by happenstance. But that is not true because your rise to empress was all due to your own actions."

I am stunned into silence. To hear such things from the emperor himself is unbelievable. Is it possible that what he says is true? I might not be the Daughter of Heaven. I am not even Manchu. But the emperor is truly the Son of Heaven. He is the emissary of the gods, the mouth of the ancestors. If he believes that I am the rightful empress, it must be true! Tears of joy and relief fall from my eyes.

"Have I upset you?" he asks, reaching for my hand.

"No," I say. "Quite the opposite. You have made me very happy."

He chuckles and squeezes my hands in his, looking into my eyes. "I love you, Lihua."

My heart thuds so hard I think it will crack out of my chest. The use of my name—of another girl's name—completely unravels the words of reassurance that came before. He only believes that I am meant to be here because he doesn't know the truth. He doesn't know who I am. If he did, this man who claims to love me would see my head cut from my body.

I realize he is looking at me expectantly, waiting for a response to the words he just used. I slip from my seat and kneel by his side.

"You have honored me above all women, first by making me empress, and then by giving me the gift of your love. I am incredibly blessed to have my feelings of love returned."

He smiles and tugs me back to my seat. He smiles so that the edges of his eyes crinkle, but there are tears there too. Tears of joy, I fear. I could not say the words he wanted to hear, "I love you, too." Because I don't. He is kind to me, certainly. He is an enjoyable lover. And his affection keeps me safe and secure for now. But I do not love him. I suppose I should feel guilty about this. How many women are sold to cold and cruel husbands every day? How many women live and die without hearing such words of affection? But I cannot deny my own feelings.

I care for the emperor very much. He makes me happy. Spoils me. Should some calamity befall him, I would grieve the loss of him. Grieve the loss of the best emperor China could possibly have. But I would not grieve him as a husband.

Thoughts of Honghui—the emperor's brother—come to my mind unbidden. I do not allow myself to think of him, yet he pushes into my thoughts far too often. Honghui is who I love, and the knowledge brings me great sorrow. We can never be together. I have not even seen him since I became empress, and I doubt I will ever see him again.

All of these thoughts and feelings are racing through me, and Guozhi has no idea. He only looks at me with love and happiness. I lean forward and kiss him, doing my best to reassure him and hide my true feelings.

"Lihua," he whispers when our lips part.

"Hmm?"

"I really am very hungry."

"Oh!" I had forgotten for a moment the true purpose of his visit. "I'm so sorry." I quickly fill a bowl with items from around the table and then give him a bowl of rice. I ladle him a bowl of soup and refill his teacup.

He laughs. "Sit, sit, you silly girl, and eat with me."

I find that my hand is no longer shaking and that I am rather hungry as well. We eat in companionable silence for a time and I wonder if I am perhaps overthinking things. I suppose it might no longer matter where I came from. I am here now. I cannot change the past, nor can I predict the future. Would it be possible for me to be happy, at least for a time? And should my past catch up to me, I will face whatever comes with as much dignity as I can muster. I only hope it will be enough.

"How are you settling in as empress?" Guozhi asks me.

"I think it is going well," I say. "I...I still do not feel up to the task all the time, but I am seeking help where I can find it. Lady Euhmeh was trained by Lady An to maintain the accounts, so I have put her in charge of them for now. I hope to eventually learn enough to oversee her, but for now, I have to trust what she says."

Guozhi nods, but his face is grim. "Do not put too much trust in the other concubines. They will be jealous of you and seek to undermine your authority. And their mistakes will fall upon you as head of the harem."

"What should I do?" I ask. "I am not smart enough to know whether what she says is true or false."

He smirks. "You need to learn to leverage your position."

I shrug. Everyone keeps telling me this, but I hardly know how to.

"You have great authority, and plenty of money. I heard that you elevated two of your ladies to rank-three consorts."

"I hope I have not angered you," I say.

He waves me off and shakes his head. "No, but that is only a fraction of what you could do. Here is what I suggest. Appoint a second lady to oversee the accounts, one who can check the work of the first, and Euhmeh can check the other lady's work as well. Tell them that it is to improve accuracy if two eyes examine the entries."

I nod, but I am still unclear as to how having two women I don't know handling the accounts will help me.

"Then, whenever your ladies, any of them, please you, reward them generously—openly, so that all may see. You will see people vying for your favor. Working to make you happy. That way, if either girl makes an error with the accounts, the second one will report her dutifully. It will also make them afraid to try and make errors in their own favor since they know they will be caught."

I nod slowly. "I think I understand. The women will be loyal to me if they know they will be rewarded for it. But they will also be afraid to make any intentional errors because they know they will be caught."

"Exactly," Guozhi says. "See, you are more clever than you know. You learn quickly."

"Thank you for the advice," I say.

We are quiet a little longer as we eat a bit more. "There is one more thing," I say. He nods for me to continue. "I am sorry that I have not yet given you a son. If his majesty will allow it, I would like to be responsible for raising your children."

He looks at me for a long moment, and I fear that he will become angry. The last time we fought, it was over Dongmei, Lady An's daughter. But eventually he nods.

"You are their mother," he says. "Do as you will."

My heart skips a beat. "Thank you. But...your mother, the dowager, she and I do not always agree on what is best for them. What should I do?"

"You must give your mother-in-law the respect she deserves," he says. "But *you* are their mother. The final decisions regarding their welfare fall to you."

My heart is racing, but I know I cannot be overconfident. The dowager will not be happy when I try to make decisions for the girls.

"So, you will support me in this?" I say. "Should your mother and I disagree, you will support my decisions."

"Matters of the harem should not fall at my door," he says, growing irritated. "I have enough to worry about without petty jealousies and arguments needing my attention."

I sigh in disappointment. This is not enough of a reassurance for me. "Of course, your majesty."

"However," he goes on, to my surprise, "you are young, and new to your position. Should you need my support as you learn to navigate your new place as empress, you will have it."

I am so happy I can hardly contain myself as I try to thank him. He laughs as he stands, pulling me along with him. He holds me in his arms and we kiss. We start to move toward my bed-chamber when we are interrupted by Fiyanggu.

"Forgive me, your majesties," he says, "but there is an urgent matter that requires the emperor's attention."

"What is it that cannot wait until morning?" Guozhi asks.

"It is regarding the negotiations—" Fiyanggu starts to say, but the emperor cuts him off, instantly aware of what the eunuch is talking about.

"Can I not have an hour of peace?" he says.

"What is wrong?" I ask.

"Nothing that needs concern you," Guozhi says. "But I am afraid I must go."

"Of course," I say. Guozhi kisses me again.

"I will return for dinner tomorrow night," he says, then he and his servants exit the courtyard, leaving the house feeling surprisingly empty.

I wonder what negotiations he is so worried about, but I suppose I will never know. I truly have no idea what is happening outside the walls of the harem. Are we at war? Peace? Is there a drought or a failed harvest? Are we living in a golden age of plenty? I shake my head to erase such thoughts. Such matters do not concern me, so I should not worry. Whatever happens outside, I know the emperor will keep me safe.

6

"Lihua!" Jiangfei cries out as she runs into my arms. I drop to my knees and hold her tightly. Dongmei, always the more reserved one, is right behind her, and I hold both girls close. They are not my children, but I love them like my own little sisters.

"I've missed you so much," Jiangfei says. "Where have you been?"

"I've been right here," I say.

"Then why haven't we seen you?" Dongmei asks, worry on her face.

"I'm sorry," I say. I don't want to tell them that the dowager empress had all but forbidden me from seeing the girls. For some reason, the dowager doesn't think I should have much of a say in how the girls are raised. But after my conversation with Guozhi, I am confident that Fenfeng will not be able to stop me from being a surrogate mother to the girls—as is my right as empress.

"Ever since...since I became empress, there have been a lot of changes around here. I needed time to adjust. But everything is settled now, and I have good news."

"What is it?" Jiangfei asks.

"You will be moving to the palace right next to mine," I say. "That way we can always be close."

"Yay!" Jiangfei says. "I want to see. Can I pick my room? Is there a pond?"

Jiangfei is already at the gate of my courtyard. Dongmei, however, seems apprehensive. I hold my hand out to her.

"Do you want to see?"

She nods and takes my hand. We all—including the crowd of servants that follow me everywhere nowadays— walk the short distance along my courtyard wall that turns into the courtyard wall for the princess's palace to the gate of the girls' new home.

"Ducks!" Jiangfei says, rushing into the courtyard to the pond where a couple of ducks and few ducklings have made their home.

"They apparently moved in while the palace was empty and I did not have the heart to throw them out," I say. "They leave a lot of poop around, though, so you must be careful where you step."

Jiangfei tries to pet one of the larger ducks, but it waddles into the pond to escape her touch. When she manages to grab one of the yellow ducklings, the other large duck runs over, quacking up a storm and raising her wings wide. Jiangfei shrieks and drops the duckling, running to me to protect her.

"Why are they so mean?" she asks.

"They just need time to get to know you," I say. "You must be gentle with them and very quiet. Why don't you ask Cook for some bread to feed them."

All of the palaces have similar layouts, so Jiangfei runs in the direction of the kitchen. I turn to Dongmei and squeeze her hands.

"What do you think?" I ask. "Will you be happy here?"

She shrugs.

"What's wrong?" I ask her, leading her to a small round table. I ask one of the servants to bring some sweet treats and tea.

"I wonder how long we will be allowed to stay here," she says.

"As long as you like," I say, trying to reassure her. "Well, until your father arranges a marriage for you, but that is still some years away."

She sighs and looks away.

"I thought you would be happy to be closer to me," I say. "We can visit each other all the time. We can paint and embroider together, or whatever you like."

"Until Grandmother moves us," she says.

"What are you talking about?"

She is quiet for a moment as she stares off at nothing. "First, Mother An died, and I was moved to a smaller palace. Then Mother died and Grandmother moved us both closer to her. Grandmother sent all our servants and tutors away and hired new ones. She told Jiangfei and me that we shouldn't spend so much time with you. That you are just a poor, country girl and know nothing about being a lady. I am sure Grandmother will come and move us again soon."

My heart breaks for my poor little girl. I have been through so much these few months, but Dongmei has been through more. Jiangfei as well, but she is little and doesn't seem to understand everything that is going on around her. I lost my family, but I left them willingly, and I believe they are safe—wherever they are. I often think of my rise to the position of empress as a curse. Something I do not want that will surely lead to a bad end. But in reality, it has been a blessing of sorts. I have money and food, plenty of servants, a large home, and the love of the emperor. I can hardly complain. But Dongmei... Poor Dongmei.

I pull Dongmei to my lap and hold her tightly. "You will not have to move again, I promise. Your father has said that I am your mother now. And you know his word is law."

She lays her head on my shoulder and hugs me back. "I hope so."

"Dongmei!" Jiangfei runs over and hands a steamed bun to her sister. "Come on."

Dongmei slips from my lap and goes with her sister to the pond to feed the ducks and koi. A lot of the anxiety that had marked Dongmei's face seems to melt away as she plays with her sister. I hope I have put some of her worries to rest.

Dongmei is smart and observant. She is right to think that Fenfeng will try to put an end to my meddling. I am sure she will. But Guozhi has assured me that he will support me first when it comes to raising the girls, and I believe he will keep his word. He has always been truthful and honest with me, which is more than I can say about myself. He's a far better husband than I deserve...

A eunuch announces that Euhmeh has arrived. I have barely gotten to my feet when she is stomping across the courtyard, her lips pinched tight. She remembers her manners, though, and gives a small bow when she reaches me.

"What brings you here?" I ask, though I already know the answer.

"Is it true that you appointed Samala Qiao to manage the accounts as well?" she asks.

"Yes," I say. "Qiao was very well-educated back home. I'm sure she will be a great help to you."

"I don't need any help," Euhmeh says. "Have I made any mistakes? Have I been dishonest in my accounting?"

"No," I say. "Of course not. You have done very well."

"Then, why?"

"It was a suggestion by his majesty," I say, and her eyes go wide. I think she might cry.

"His majesty is disappointed with me?"

"No! Not at all. It's me. I am very stupid when it comes to numbers. I could never do half of what you are able to. The emperor thought it would help me if I had two people to help manage the accounts."

Euhmeh's lips press tightly and she looks away for a moment. "Of course, his majesty is wise in all things. Whatever he says must be correct."

"I agree," I say.

"But I don't need help," Euhmeh says, her voice tight. "I don't need a spy looking over my shoulder."

"What?" I ask dumbly. "A spy? What do you mean?"

"A farm cannot have two roosters," she says. "I only helped Lady An with recording numbers. I was never her equal. I did not do the calculations or report to the empress. The accounts have never been managed by two people."

I am unsure of what to say. Euhmeh is very smart, and not only when it comes to numbers. I had hoped that she wouldn't know why I was giving her a partner, or that she would be humble enough not to question me about it. I can't imagine ever questioning one of Caihong's decisions. This thought gives me strength.

"How dare you question my motives," I say, my voice strong. Her eyes go wide. "Am I not the empress? Are you not a lowly, rank-five concubine?"

Euhmeh tries to reply, but she cannot find the words.

She drops down to her knees. "I am sorry, your majesty. Please, punish me how you see fit."

I hadn't thought about punishing her. I really don't want to. I only wanted to stop her from arguing with me. I look around the courtyard for help, but I only see servants watching, waiting to see what I will do. Whatever happens, gossip of it will spread through the inner court like wildfire. I have no desire to humiliate Euhmeh, but I must do something. I look down at her, still kneeling before me.

"You will go outside my gate and kneel for the rest of the day," I say. "You may leave at sunset."

I see her jaw clench before she kowtows before me. "Yes, your majesty." Her maid helps her to stand and they back away from me, toward the gate. They step outside and start walking to the left.

"Where I can see you!" I yell after them. They are immediately back in front of the gate, where Euhmeh kneels, her head bowed. I look up at the spring sun and am glad that there are only a couple of hours of daylight left. I walk over to a bench under the courtyard awning and pick up a puffy pillow. I motion Suyin toward me.

"Give her this," I say.

"Are you sure, my lady?" she asks. "She is being punished, not pampered,"

"I am not cruel," I say, thrusting the pillow at her. Suyin presses her lips but does as I command. I see her help Euhmeh onto the pillow, and then I move to where I can't see Euhmeh. I don't want to watch her humiliation. It was necessary, but I take no joy in it.

I have barely made it back to the duck pond with the girls when it is announced that Dowager Empress Fenfeng has arrived. Can I not get a moment's peace? Everyone in the courtyard falls to their knees except for me, Dongmei, and Jiangfei. We only bow.

"Welcome, Mother," I say.

"What is going on?" she asks. "What have you done to Lady Euhmeh?"

"I have done nothing to her," I say. "She was insolent. She will be allowed to leave at sunset."

She is clearly displeased, but she says nothing more on the matter. I am surprised that Fenfeng even knows Euhmeh's name. Is Euhmeh a special pet to her?

"I have heard that you have moved the princesses away from me," she goes on.

"I wanted them closer to me," I say, "since I am their mother now."

"Don't be ridiculous," Fenfeng says. "You are barely more than a child yourself. You cannot possibly know how to raise the girls."

"I am the empress," I say. "They are my children by right."

Fenfeng scoffs and she steps closer to me, lowering her voice. "You are only the empress because I allow it to be so. Do you not think that one word from me to my son would send you back to rank six? Or even back to the home of your mother?"

My mouth goes dry and I tremble a little. Of course, all people are supposed to honor the will and wishes of their parents. Is it possible that Guozhi will defer to his mother and break his vow to me? I fear it is possible. I consider humbling myself before her. Begging her not to take the girls from me. I would do whatever it takes to protect them and keep them near to me.

I see Dongmei out of the corner of my eye. Tears are already running down her cheeks as she watches us. I promised her mere minutes ago that she would not have to move again. I promised, and she dared to hope it would be true. The first bit of stability she has touched in months is about to be ripped away from her. I cannot let that happen. I step back and speak clearly for all to hear.

"I thank you for your wise counsel, Mother. But as empress, I will decide what is best for the children from now on."

Fenfeng's face darkens so much, I think it starts to block out the sun. "You are going to regret this. I will go and see my son about the matter right now."

"I am the head of the harem," I say. "Any concerns you have should go through me."

"You insolent, little bug!" she hisses at me. "I'll have your tongue for this."

I swallow in the face of a threat of bodily harm, but I'll not give in. I will not let Dongmei think that I did not fight for her should the emperor abandon me. I say nothing, and Fenfeng whirls around, turning her back on me—on her empress—as she leaves the courtyard. It is a grave insult, but one I choose to ignore.

"Come," I tell Dongmei and Jiangfei, "let us work on your embroidery."

We work in tense silence in the courtyard. I expect the emperor to appear at any moment and chastise me for speaking against his mother. But as the sun sets and I see Euhmeh rise to her feet and her maid help her totter away back to her own palace, the emperor does not come.

And neither does the dowager.

7
—————

"They say the dowager is furious," Suyin whispers to me as she styles my hair for the day.

"Really?" I ask, though I can't help but preen a bit like a fat cat. I haven't seen Fenfeng for days except during the morning greetings. And even then, she hasn't spoken to me.

"The emperor told her that you were the mother of his children and that the girls should answer to you."

"As I expected," I say. "He told me the very same. I was a little concerned that he would not keep his word in the face of his mother's wrath, but I am pleased he did. What did Fenfeng say in response?"

"She was displeased, of course," Suyin says, folding my hair around a bian fang. "Said that you were not fit to raise imperial princesses. But he dismissed her concerns with a mere wave of his hand."

I chuckle. "She can't have been too happy about that."

"Certainly not, but she wouldn't dare defy her son. She conceded and returned to her palace without another word. She hasn't spoken to anyone outside of her palace since, but her maids say that she is brooding. She blames you for losing power over the harem and influence over the emperor. She seems to think you are her enemy."

"Enemy," I scoff. "This is not a war. Not a battle where two foes must fight to the bitter end. She is my mother-in-law. If she did not try to usurp my authority, did not try to take the girls from me, then I would gladly accept her as a friend. Does she not see that?"

Suyin shakes her head as she pins several jewels to my wide liangbatou. It is strange how accustomed I have become to wearing the silly fan on the top of my head. I used to dread it, but now I hardly notice it is there. The same with walking on pot-bottom shoes. Of course, I still cannot run or walk on uneven surfaces. But in the safety of the palace, balancing on top of the shoes and swinging my feet as I walk has become second nature.

I shrug. "Well, let's just hope that her temper cools eventually and she sees reason in being friends."

"Yes, my lady," Suyin says.

I hesitate. "But...if you do hear anything that I should know about, do tell me."

"Yes, your majesty."

I know that there is much jealousy among the women in the harem. I expect it from the concubines and consorts. But I never thought I would clash with the emperor's mother. I remember the time I saw Fenfeng and Lady An talking secretly in a garden. I forget the details now, but it was about Empress Caihong. Somehow, and for some reason I cannot understand, Fenfeng tried to elevate Lady An above Caihong in the emperor's affection. It didn't work, of course. The emperor never had any feelings for Lady An, while he was completely in love with Caihong. Still, I wouldn't put it past Fenfeng to try to find ways to undermine my position as well. If she does, I would like to know about it so I can defend myself.

As I leave my palace, Yanmei is waiting for me, but Wangli is not. "Where is she?" I ask.

"She said she wasn't feeling well," Yanmei says. "She received some bad news from home."

"What sort of bad news?"

She shakes her head. "I don't know. She didn't tell me."

"Hmm. Odd. You would think that if a family member was ill or something she would tell one of us. I wonder what it is."

"Would you like me to ask around?" Suyin offers helpfully.

"No," I tell her. "I'll call on her as soon as morning greetings are over."

~

My arrival at Wangli's palace is announced by one of my many eunuch servants. Wangli and all of her household rush into the courtyard and kneel.

"I am sorry I did not greet you this morning, my lady," Wangli says. "I was unwell."

I wave my hand to dismiss the servants and they quickly scatter. Wangli stands up and faces me. She looks terrible. Her eyes are puffy and her cheeks are red. She has clearly been crying. I take her arm in mine as we walk to one of her sitting rooms.

"What is wrong?" I ask. "Has someone taken ill? Is it your mother?"

"No," she says as she pulls a letter out of one of her sleeve pockets. "It's my brother, the one nearest in age to me, Tongtong."

I nod as I wait for her to continue.

"He's been conscripted into military service," she says in a whisper. I shake my head dumbly. "He's been ordered to join the army."

"Ordered?" I ask. "By whom?"

"By the emperor," she says.

"No," I say. "That cannot be. Why would the emperor do such a thing?"

Wangli sniffs. "Apparently, we are at war."

My stomach freezes in my gut. "War?" I can hardly believe what I am hearing. How could we be at war? And with whom? And why would the emperor need more soldiers than the army already has? I have so many questions but no idea who to turn to for answers.

"What does the letter say exactly? Tell me everything."

"Mother says that since Tongtong is unmarried—all three others have wives and children—he must report for military service by the end of the week. She says that—" She lowers her voice. "—that we are being invaded by foreigners."

My head starts to spin. Foreign invaders! Hundreds of years ago the Manchu were foreign invaders. They overthrew the Chinese emperor and set up their own empire here in our country. Could the same thing be happening again? A new foreign power invading us and setting themselves up as leaders? The thought makes me sick.

I thought it odd at first that Wangli was whispering. But now I see why. This is terrible, frightening news. I would not want the servants or ladies of the harem to be worried by such information. I keep my voice low as well.

"Did she say where the foreigners were from? From the north?"

"She didn't say exactly where, only that they were from across the sea."

I shake my head. I know nothing of the world outside China. Outside Peking, to be honest. They could be from anywhere.

"But, they have invaded already?" I ask. "Where? When? Why have we not heard anything?"

"I don't know," Wangli says. Her eyes well up again and she cries into her hands.

"It will be all right," I say, putting my arm around her. "I am sure it is only a lot of posturing, but nothing real. The emperor just needs a show of force. He needs to show that we cannot be overrun so easily."

"Do you think so?" Wangli asks.

I nod, but in truth, I have no idea what is happening. We could be in a dire situation and I would never know.

"Don't worry until we have more information," I say, wiping the tears from her face with my sleeve. "I'll try to speak to the emperor about this. Learn what is happening."

"Do you think...do you think that you could ask the emperor to spare my brother? The army must have thousands of men in it. Surely the emperor could spare one."

I don't like what Wangli is asking of me. It doesn't seem like my place to speak to the emperor about something happening outside the red walls. Wangli must read the hesitation on my face.

"No, of course you couldn't," she says, looking away. "You don't even know him. Why should you stick your neck out for a stranger?"

"It's not that," I try to explain. "Not exactly. I have no idea what is going on. I would hate to ask the emperor to do something that might not even be necessary. I...I don't want to look foolish."

Wangli nods. "I understand. Maybe you are right and I am fretting for nothing."

"The next time I speak to the emperor, I will ask about the war. Hopefully he will put all our fears to rest."

"Yes," Wangli says. "That is a good idea. No sense speculating, I suppose."

"Exactly. Though, I am sorry for your family's distress. I would like to send them a gift. Even if your brother comes home safe and sound, it must be a burden for your parents to not have him at home. Perhaps a bit of extra money will help relieve the stress."

"You are too kind, my lady," she says, her eyes going wide for a moment as if in horror. "But my family is comfortable. And my other brothers are still there. They will be fine, I am sure."

I wonder if I have insulted her by offering to send money to her parents. I suppose I must have. As my lady's maid and a rank-three concubine, her income is one of the largest of the harem. She must have plenty of money to send home.

I think about my family and wonder if this war will affect them. Will Father be ordered to join the army? No, surely not. Wangli said that her brother had been selected because he was unmarried. He has no family of his own relying on him. Father has a wife and many children. Wherever he is, I am sure he is safe. But I then think of my old hutong neighborhood. So many people lived as we did, able to earn only enough money each day to buy food to survive. Missing a single day of work meant a family would go hungry that day. It happened to us often enough. Any one of the families near us would suffer greatly if someone was taken away.

"There must be other families that will suffer if their son

is taken away. Especially families with only one son. I wonder if there is anything I could do to help."

"What about your collections for poor relief?" Wangli asks. "The thing you were working on with Prince Honghui."

Panic washes over me at the mention of Honghui's name. I do my best to quickly wash it away and pray my feelings didn't show on my face. If anyone even suspected that I had feelings for the prince, the emperor could throw me over—or worse.

"Oh, yes," I say. "The prince delivered the money directly into the hands of the poor. He said that the people were very grateful. I suppose I could do something like that again, collect money to send to the families of soldiers."

"You didn't collect much before, though, did you?" Wangli says. "It was mostly your own money."

"Yes, that is true. I felt embarrassed asking the other ladies to donate their allowance. I know that many of them support their families back home already. And some have a lot of expenses here."

"I'll help you this time," she says. "If there is a war, the people will suffer greatly. We can surely do with a little less food or one less winter gown if it will help keep people from starving."

"I agree! It is a thought very near to my heart that I have so much while the people of Peking have so little. I don't need half of what I have."

"The prince should be able to help you again," she says. "He will surely know which families the soldiers are taken from."

I hate the idea of seeking out Honghui's company, but I cannot deny that she is right. The prince has always supported my efforts to give money to the people. Of course, he has no idea why. No idea that not so very long ago, I was living on the streets and could have used a bit of cash.

"I still need to speak to the emperor first," I say. "It would not be right of me to go to the prince first. I will speak to him tonight when he joins me for dinner."

8

The emperor did not come to my palace for supper that night, nor for many nights after. Neither did he call me to his bed. But he was not alone.

Suyin informed me that he had spent several nights with Euhmeh.

"How did Euhmeh come to be called to his bed?" I asked. "She's a rank-five concubine. The chance that he would choose her from all the others is quite small."

"I heard that it was Empress Dowager Fenfeng who suggested her to him," Suyin says.

"Why would she do that?" I ask. I remember that Fenfeng knew Euhmeh by name when she saw her outside my palace. Why would the empress take such notice of someone so low-ranking?

"She seemed to have gotten to know Euhmeh when she was Lady An's assistant," Suyin explains.

"Is that all?" I ask. Suyin shrugs. It is all very strange to me. Still, none of that is as disconcerting as the fact that Guozhi has spent several nights with Euhmeh instead of only one before selecting someone else—or coming to me.

"The emperor is...pleased with Euhmeh?" I ask.

"It seems so," Suyin says. "He has sent her many gifts. And..." She hesitates.

"And...?" I prod.

"And it is rumored that he will elevate her to rank four."

"Is she with child?" I ask.

"Not yet," Suyin says. "At least, there are no signs that she is."

I sit back in my chair and sigh. I don't understand it. I don't want to mistrust Euhmeh. I had hoped that we would become friends. Though, it seems that by taking Guozhi's advice and appointing a second lady to help manage the harem finances, I ruined any chance of that. And punishing her that one day for insolence probably made the dowager like me even less. I wonder just how many mistakes I've made since becoming empress. How many enemies I've made.

I ask Fiyanggu, the head of household affairs, to tell the emperor that I needed to speak to him urgently. To my surprise, the emperor calls me to his small audience hall, not the large official audience hall with the dragon throne, but a smaller one he uses for daily meetings with his closest advisors.

When I arrive, we are not alone. Prince Honghui is there, as are a couple of other men I do not know. One looks to be a military man of some sort, a general, I suppose. The rest are all members of the emperor's council I have seen from time to time. I am a little nervous around so many men. I had thought the emperor would speak to me privately.

I bow to the emperor when I enter the room. "Thank you for agreeing to see me, your majesty."

"Yes, yes. I am sorry I have not been to see you," he says.

"My duties as emperor have taken much of my time lately. I will visit you soon, I promise."

"Wives, even empresses, can hardly go a single day without constant attention, apparently," one of the men says with a laugh. The other men, except for the emperor and Honghui, follow suit.

"That's not it at all," I say, focusing on the emperor. "The women of the harem have been receiving letters from home, as they always do. But the letters lately speak of unrest, even war. The women are frightened for their families. I have tried to reassure them, tell them that no matter what happens, you will protect us. But I feel compelled to ask if what they say is true. Are we at war?"

Guozhi rubs his chin as he looks at me.

"Leave it to clucking hens to fret over matters that don't concern them," someone says.

"Silence," Guozhi tells the man. He then sighs as he looks at me. "I would not want to cause you concern. We are not at open war, but there have been hostilities between our empire and countries from the East."

"Countries?" I ask, afraid. "More than one?"

Guozhi waves his hand as if this detail is not important. "No one power could ever defeat the great Qing Dynasty! They must join forces to even have a chance at such an endeavor."

"Is that what they have done?" I ask. "Foreign powers have joined forces against us?"

I expect Guozhi to lie to me, to give me more false reassurances. And I think he considers it, but he seems to change his mind.

"War will probably come soon," he says. "But you need not worry about your safety. War will never breach the walls of the Forbidden City."

I am afraid, but I cannot act so, or the emperor will refuse to tell me anything more.

"What should we do, then?" I ask.

"There is nothing the women of the harem can do," he says. "But as empress, it is your responsibility to keep the women calm and reassured. It will not do to have the women in hysterics. I need to focus on matters outside the inner court."

"Yes, of course," I say. "I understand. But if there is any way we can help, please tell me. If we should donate to help the families of the men who have been pressed into serving in the army, we would gladly do so."

Guozhi considers this for a moment. "Yes, I think this is a fine idea. You should gather as many funds as you can. Honghui will collect them."

I bend my knees and bow. "Thank you, your majesty. I would hate to feel useless at such a time."

"It would be far better for me if you remain as you are," Guozhi says. "Time in the inner court, nights with my ladies, these are times when I do not wish to be bothered with business affairs. Keep the women reassured so they do not pester me about such matters."

"Yes, your majesty," I say. "Thank you for agreeing to speak with me."

He nods and dismisses me. I back out of the room and let out a breath I must have been holding for some time.

China is at war! And against many foes. Despite the emperor's words, I do not believe that this is a small matter easily overcome. The fighting might not breach the walls of the Forbidden City, but should the emperor be defeated, what will become of me, his empress? Of all of his women?

I place my hand on the wall to steady myself. The fear makes my knees weak. I feel helpless. Gathering funds will do nothing to help keep us safe should the worst happen. What should I do?

I hear the door to the audience hall open and close behind me and I stand up straight and continue my walk down the hall toward my waiting sedan chair.

"Lihua!" I look back to see Honghui coming toward me.

"I am not of the mind to talk about fundraising at the moment," I say.

"I'm sure," he says. "I had a feeling you were not fooled by my brother's words."

My stomach sours. "Things are worse than he said, then."

"Very," he says. "We have a large standing army, yes. But the foreigners are not fighting on land, not yet. They have ships, lots of them. The coastal towns are being devastated."

My hand goes to my mouth and I have to lean against the wall again. People are already dying in this conflict and I had no idea. Father had talked about moving to the coast, to one of the shipping docks where there was more work. Surely, after all the money Mingxia gave them for me, they did not go through with that plan. But they could have moved anywhere!

"Please," Honghui says, placing a hand on my arm. "Do not cry."

I pull my arm from his grasp. "I'm not crying. I'm angry! I'm... Fine, yes, I'm afraid. But why wasn't I told? Why has Guozhi *still* not told me the truth? There must be something I should be doing. The shipping ports are not far from Peking. What if we *are* invaded? Should we not move somewhere safer now, just in case?"

"Yes," Honghui says. "You should be moved. I told my brother that you should all be sent to the Winter Palace, up north in the city of Jehol, but he has not listened to me, not yet."

My mouth gapes. Even though I said it first, I did not expect Honghui to agree with me. I thought he would tell me that I was overreacting. I rub my forehead, feeling faint.

"But what can I do?" I ask. "I—we, the women—we cannot just leave. Guozhi would not allow it." I almost have to chuckle to myself at the memory of me climbing a tree to escape the Forbidden City. I wonder if I should attempt it again. Get myself out if no one else. No, I couldn't do that. I couldn't leave the others behind.

"No, but you can prepare for the worst," Honghui says. "Pack a trunk with your most essential items. Your clothes, your jewels, anything small of great value. A trunk that you could grab at a moment's notice should you have to flee."

"You cannot be serious," I say, even though I know he is. But the idea that we might have to leave Peking suddenly is too terrifying to think about. "The women will panic if I order them to pack trunks for an escape."

"That is why you must not tell them," Honghui says, his face stern.

"I cannot leave them in the dark—"

"Yes, you can," he says. "And you must. And if needs be...you have to leave them behind."

"What?" I'm almost disgusted by the suggestion—even though I thought something not too dissimilar only moments ago. But I would never have said such a thing aloud! "No! I can't—"

"You are the empress," he says. "You are worth all the others put together."

"That is not true," I say.

"To the foreigners, it is very much true," he says. "They don't understand our ways. They believe that a man—even a king—has only one wife. In their eyes, you are the only woman who matters to Guozhi."

"I don't understand," I say. "What is your meaning?"

"If the foreigners were to get their hands on you, it would be very bad for all of us."

"Get their... What? You mean kidnap me?"

"Yes," he says. "Or take you hostage in some other manner."

"But I still don't understand. What would taking me hostage accomplish? I'm not involved in any of this. I have no say over politics or war."

"Guozhi would never let anything bad happen to you," Honghui says.

"That's... I don't..." I take a breath as I try to understand what Honghui is telling me. "If something were to happen to me, Guozhi would simply replace me, just like how I replaced Caihong."

"Not in a case like this," he says. "If he were to let the foreigners have you, it would be a great disgrace. He would be seen as weak and heartless by the foreigners if he did not protect his wife. Even more countries might join their cause if they think that Guozhi is that cruel."

I shake my head. "This is madness! Guozhi would never risk losing a war become of me. If I were Caihong, an empress he truly loved, maybe. And while the emperor says he loves me, I know it is not true."

"He...he has told you that he's in love with you?" Honghui asks, his brow furrowed. There is a confusion, a sadness on his face.

"I do not think he means it," I say. "I think he has affection for me. That he cares for me. But love? No, not really."

"Hmm." Honghui looks away for a moment and I wonder what he is thinking. I was already his brother's wife when we made love. Why would his brother's declaration that he loved me seem to bother Honghui more than me being his brother's wife?

"Besides," I go on, trying to steer the conversation back to where it needs to be, "even if he did, I am only a woman. He would not risk his country to save me."

"Perhaps," Honghui says. "But we must be prepared for any possible outcome. If keeping you safe is one less way the foreigners might gain an advantage over us, then that is what we must do."

"Fine," I say. "Then what should I do? Guozhi will not hide me elsewhere. You already said as much."

"Not yet," he says. "But should things take a turn for the worst, he will. And you must be ready to leave at a moment's notice."

"I will do as you suggest. I will prepare for departure."

"But *don't* tell the other women," he reiterates. "We cannot have the palace fall into panic and chaos."

"But, my ladies. My friends—"

"No one!" he says.

What he asks is impossible. If I have to flee, I would not leave Wangli or Yanmei behind. But there is no sense in arguing.

"As for the money—"

"What money?"

He looks at me for a moment, waiting, and then my face blushes.

"Oh, yes. The money I am supposed to be raising for the families of soldiers. In truth, I only came up with the plan as an excuse to take to Guozhi about what was going on."

"Good," he says. "Because none of that money will go to the people."

"Why?"

"My brother will use it to fund the war."

"Oh," I say. "Should I just do nothing, then?"

"Gather as much as you can," he says. "And hide it. Keep it on you, hide it in your trunk. Bury it in the garden if you must. If you have to flee, you might wish you had that money available to you instead of given to the people."

There is urgency in his words. An urgency motivated by fear. I only now notice the beads of sweat on his forehead, the wild look in his eyes, his unkempt hair. It is as if he has not slept in days, and he probably hasn't. This is all new information to me, but Honghui has been privy to this information from the beginning. He has watched this situation go from bad to worse—and he's not confident about what will happen next.

From the day I set foot in the Forbidden City, I have been afraid. I have lived every day with the possibility of being discovered and being put to death. I never imagined that the biggest threat to my safety might come from outside the palace walls.

I know I should go. Start my preparations for having to flee. Find a way to save my friends. But I am hesitant to leave this spot. Right now, I feel frozen. As if the war, the danger, isn't here yet, but will storm through the doors as soon as I step back inside the inner court. As long as I stay where I am, I feel as though I can keep that from happening.

Honghui seems reluctant to leave as well. But we cannot stand here forever. He reaches up and touches my face.

"Whatever happens," he says, "I will keep you safe. I promise."

I shake my head. "Don't say that. Things are so far out of our control, we should not make promises we might not be able to keep."

He starts to protest, but I step to him, pulling on the collar of his robe to bring his face to mine. There are no more words to say. No more promises to make. Whatever happens next will happen whether we will it to or not.

But I am not without hope. As I take in Honghui's scent, his touch, I remember that not all is lost. The war has not yet reached us, and even if it does, China is a vast country. We could flee the city and no one would ever be able to find us. Honghui and I could run away together... Finally be together...

He pulls away from the kiss first.

"I must get back," he says. "Guozhi needs me. I think that we should try to negotiate, come to some sort of peace terms. But his other counselors..." He shakes his head. "They seem to welcome war to our shores."

"Go, then," I tell him, stepping back. "Do not worry about me. Not now. I can take care of myself."

He smirks and taps me on the nose. "I believe that. I have a feeling that even if all of China should fall, somehow, you would still be left standing."

"Let's hope it does not come to that."

His smile falters at the reminder of our grim situation. He gives me a small bow and then returns to the audience hall. I take a few calming breaths and continue toward my waiting sedan chair. I have much to do and no idea how much time I have to do it.

9

"Close the door," I tell Jinhai after I invite him and Suyi to my bed-chamber. I am pacing, wringing my hands. I cannot prepare to leave on my own. My servants must help me. Even if I were to try and prepare in secret, they would notice when things go missing.

"What I have to tell you must be held in the strictest confidence," I tell them.

"Of course, your majesty," Suyin says. "We would never—"

"No," I say. "I am serious. This is not like past times where you whisper secrets among your closest friends and make bargains for information. If this information gets out, I will not be able to protect you from the consequences."

They exchange glances and then nod. "Yes, my lady," Suyin says. "You can trust us."

"I know, but I cannot take any chances. I must be clear about this. Not a word."

They both agree and step a little closer to me. I lower my voice to a whisper. "We must prepare to flee the Forbidden City."

Jinhai gasps and Suyin whimpers.

"Because of the war?" Jinhai asks. "What is happening?"

"What do you know?" Suyin asks.

"Are we safe?" Jinhai asks. Their voices rise with each question.

"Shh! We do not know who might be listening at the door. Please, lower your voices. Yes, it is because of the war. We are safe here, for now. But Prince Honghui thinks that we might need to leave soon. We are too close to the sea here. The foreigners, they have ships and are attacking the coast."

"The prince?" Suyin asks. "What of the emperor? Surely he would know better."

I shake my head. "I do not believe the emperor is being completely truthful with me. He acknowledges that the war is getting worse, but he thinks we are still safe within these walls. And maybe we are. I don't know. But Prince Honghui thinks we need to be prepared for anything, including fleeing the city if we must."

Suyin has her hand to her mouth, chewing her thumb. Jinhai is shaking but trying to remain calm. Whatever they are thinking, they are at least scared, as am I.

"Why did the prince tell you this?" Jinhai asks. "Why do his words contradict the emperor?"

"Yes, why do you believe him over the emperor?" Suyin asks.

I can feel heat rising in my cheeks. I was always very careful about sneaking out at night to see Honghui. But still, I have wondered if my servants knew that I was up to something. They are very observant and know me better than anyone. It would not have surprised me if they at least suspected my relationship with Honghui. But apparently they know nothing about it.

"I do not think that Honghui is contradicting his brother," I say. "He is only telling me what the emperor will not. Guozhi thinks that if the women of the harem find out just how dangerous the war has become, they will panic. And I think he is right. The women will be terrified."

"I don't blame them," Suyin says. "I am terrified!"

"Which is why you can't tell anyone."

"Then why are you telling us?" Jinhai asks.

"Because I need your help. Things could change at any moment. We might need to flee with almost no warning. We need to pack the essentials now so that we can grab them and leave within minutes. You should pack bags for yourself as well."

"I see," Jinhai says. "So that if we have to leave, we aren't scrambling around wasting time or end up on the road without the bare necessities."

"Exactly," I say, grateful he understands me. I take Suyin's hand. "I do not tell you any of this to frighten you, but to help you prepare. I cannot do this without you, and I would never leave you behind."

"But what about the others?" Suyin asks. "Wangli, Yanmei—"

"I have been giving it some thought," I say. "We should pack extra items. Enough for four or five ladies. Clothes and toiletries. We will not be able to pack their own items without arousing suspicion, but I have more than enough things for a dozen women. But we cannot tell the others in advance what might happen."

"I think Wangli already knows," Suyin says. "The letters from her mother—" She shakes her head. "They carry no good news."

For a moment, I consider bringing Wangli into my confidence. But I quickly dismiss the idea. Even telling my servants is a risk.

"The emperor has told me that I need to reassure the harem, keep the women calm. I will do my best. But we must prepare should the worst happen."

A few tears run down Suyin's cheeks and she hiccups. "I am so afraid."

"We have nothing to fear in this moment," I say. "The emperor still seems sure of victory, and I hope it is so. If that is the case, we might pack a few bags and cases for nothing and will have to unpack everything later. It doesn't hurt to be prepared, but we could end up in sore need if we ignore the worst possibilities."

"If we flee, where will we go?" Jinhai asks.

"The Winter Palace," I say. "I have never been there, but it is to the north and is apparently well-fortified. It is farther from the coast than we are now. Hopefully we will be safe there."

"It's an old military outpost," Jinhai says. "They call it a palace, but it is hardly as comfortable as we are here."

"As long as we are safe, we can forgo a bit of comfort," I say.

"What should we pack?" Suyin asks.

"Clothes, certainly. And a lot of them," Jinhai says. "Gowns for four or five ladies will take several trunks alone."

"I think we should pack light," I say. "We don't know how much we will be able to take with us. You should pack the plainest, simplest robes. Thin ones so that we can fit as many as possible into each trunk."

"The headdresses of course," Suyin mumbles to herself, counting items on her finger. "The phoenix crown..."

"No," I say. "No, none of that. We must pack only what

we need to survive. Clothes, shoes, some food for the journey. We don't really need much more than that. This is not a pleasure holiday."

"You're going to end up looking like a peasant," Suyin scoffs. I laugh. If only I could tell her I really was a peasant.

"A peasant who is alive," I say, rubbing her arm. "But we should take a lot of cash, and jewels. Who knows if we might end up somewhere that we will have to purchase goods."

"We should spread it out," Jinhai says. "Put the money into a lot of smaller purses and spread them out. Just in case some are stolen or lost."

"Very smart," I say. "And anything of high value that we cannot take with us, we should hide here. Bury it in the courtyard or under the stones in the floor. That way, it all will be waiting for us when we return."

Suyin starts crying harder, her shoulders shaking and her breath ragged. "I'm so frightened," she says between sobs. I put my arms around her.

"Everything will be fine, I am sure," I say. "Even the prince admitted that he was probably overreacting. He just wants to make sure we are safe."

"All of our friends," Suyin says. "The other servants. "I feel terrible not warning them."

"Suyin," I say, making my voice as stern as possible, which isn't very. "I am serious. You cannot tell anyone. There will be severe repercussions if you do."

"Yes, my lady," she says, trying to get herself back under control but not doing a very good job.

"You must start packing," I tell them. "But you must also be discreet. The other servants in the house cannot know. I don't trust them the way I trust the two of you to keep this a secret."

"That will be difficult," Jinhai says. "They are sure to notice that something is going on."

"Perhaps," I say. "But you do not have to answer any of their questions. Or you have my leave to lie if you must. I am not happy about it, but I don't know how else to avoid a panic."

"If the day comes that we will have to flee," Jinhai says, "there *will* be a panic. They will all be afraid and unprepared. You must be ready for that."

My heart is heavy at the thought. He's right. I hadn't thought about that. When the moment comes that we must flee, what will I tell the rest of the harem? How will I explain to them why I am ready to leave and they are not. How will I...leave them behind?

"I had not considered that before, but I will now. Thank you. Is there anything else?"

They glance at each other and then shake their heads.

"Very well. If at any time you have questions or concerns, tell me at once. Do not wait. But make sure we are alone."

I look at Suyin, her eyes and cheeks red and her mouth pinched with worry. "Stay here until you can collect yourself. I don't want the others to see you like this and start asking questions."

"Yes, my lady," she says.

I look to Jinhai. "Are you all right?"

"Yes, my lady," Jinhai says. "We will need time to figure out how to start packing without notice, but I am sure we will be able to sort it out."

"Good."

At that, Jinhai opens the door. I catch a glimpse of someone disappearing around a corner and the shuffling of feet. I knew that someone—or several someones—would be listening at the door. I think we kept our voices low enough, though, that they would not be able to hear anything important.

As we make our way out, a sudden fear grips my heart and I grab Jinhai's arm, pulling him back into the room.

"The children!"

His eyes go wide and Suyin's face blanches. I am disgusted with myself at the fact that I had completely forgotten about them! Honghui hadn't mentioned them to me either. He was only concerned for my safety, but they must be equally at risk. Especially Jingfei, as she is the daughter of the first empress.

I feel sick as all my careful planning comes tumbling down around me. The girls will need their own supplies, their own clothes, their own maids. But I don't know their servants well enough to trust them, and Dongmei's maids are known to be terrible gossips. The three of us return to my bed-chamber and close the door.

"What are we to do?" I ask. "How could I be so selfish?"

"You are not selfish," Suyin says. "You are anything but selfish. You have thought not only of yourself, but your friends and servants. At least you thought of the girls now and not when it was too late."

"I want the girls moved into my palace," I say. "I want them by my side at all times. I don't want to risk being separated from them if we must flee."

"That will surely arouse suspicion," Jinhai says.

I wave my hand dismissively. "There is nothing suspicious about a mother wanting to be closer to her children."

He presses his lips but says nothing. In an imperial household, it will be very suspicious for the girls not to live in their own palaces. But I can't help it. If I were to lose them, I would never forgive myself.

"What can we do to prepare the girls without others knowing?" I ask.

"I don't know that we can pack their own items without their maids knowing," Suyin says.

"Then what should we do?"

Jinhai snaps his fingers. "Bolts of cloth. We will take bolts of cloth with us and make clothes for them later."

"Indeed," Suyin says. "And they will just use your toiletries and food."

"What if we have no opportunity to sew new clothes for them?" I ask.

"We can always take in some of the larger clothes," Suyin says. "I don't think I am much bigger than Dongmei. Though, I would hate to have to dress her in servant clothes."

"Their safety is most important," I say. "They will need shoes as well."

"When they arrive here, I will find out what size they wear and find slippers in their size from among the servants," Jinhai says.

"You mean to steal them?" I ask. He shrugs, and I realize that I am hardly in a position to judge or be very picky. "Do what you must."

I sigh, letting the panic from before ease. Everything will be fine, I am sure. We have a plan. We have a place to go to. We will all be together.

We will be safe.

10

Quickly and quietly, Suyin and Jinhai pack five trunks with the most necessary of items and place them around my palace grounds. We thought it might look too conspicuous if they were all stacked together. Each trunk has a small leather pouch of coins and jewels, and there are also pouches for each of us to hide under our clothes. Jinhai loosened a floorboard in my bed-chamber, so we hid more coins and jewels under that. There is nothing left for us to do but sit, wait, and hope for the best.

I have heard no more from the emperor on the matter, so I can only hope things are going well. He also has not called me to his bed, though I suspect it is because he knows I will ask about the war and he does not want to speak of it with me. But he has called both Wangli and Yanmei, and of course Euhmeh. Since I elevated Wangli and Yanmei to rank-three concubines, they are often given precedence. The day after Yanmei is called for the first time, she is rather quiet, but there is a small smile on her face, and I think their night must have gone well. Wangli, however, is another matter.

"What is wrong?" I ask Wangli as we are sitting in the shade of a willow tree watching Dongmei and Jingfei play with a liter of long-haired kittens and their mother cat.

She lets out a sigh as she leans against the trunk of the tree, her eyes focused on something far away. There is a light breeze that waves the tassel hanging from her liangbatou. She is fingering a folded paper in her hand, another letter from home.

"I am sure the emperor is displeased with me," she says.

"Why would you think that?" I ask.

She shakes her head. "I...I think I was a disappointment to him."

I nod slowly. I remember what my maid Nuwa told me the night before I was taken to the emperor's bed for the first time. She said he liked girls who were enthusiastic, not women who were like a cold fish.

"The first night can be awkward, I know," I say. "But next time, you will know what to expect and can be better prepared."

"Next time?" she asks, then she barks a laugh. "I am sure there will not be a next time. I know what happens to women who do not satisfy him."

I nod. If the emperor finds a woman to be...poor company, he usually does not call her back again. Lady An, Dongmei's mother, was one such woman. She was only with the emperor one time and never summoned again. She was blessed to have fallen pregnant, but even that was not enough to redeem her in the emperor's eyes and she spent the rest of her nights alone. I will never forget Lady An and the troubles she faced. It was all so terribly unfair...

"I'm so torn, Lihua," Wangli goes on, then she pauses.

She looks at me before continuing. "Can I tell you something? Something in confidence?"

"Of course," I say. "I'm very good at keeping secrets."

"Do you remember the first time we met?"

"How could I forget?" It was our very first night in the Forbidden City after the consort selection. I was wide awake, so terrified and confused about how I had ended up in such a position. I heard a sound outside. When I went to investigate, I found Wangli in the garden, crying.

"I did not want to be here, did not want to be chosen," she says. "I wanted to go home to my family."

My eyes water and I pat her hand. "I understand. Truly."

"I still do not want to be called to the emperor's bed," she says. "I secretly hoped that I would live and die a maid. But at the same time, I do not wish the emperor to be angry with me."

"I understand," I say. "I was the same way. I wanted to remain hidden among the many ladies, to live a quiet life."

"That is what I thought," she says, wiping her eyes. "I thought that you and I had an understanding. But when you caught the emperor's eye..." She shakes her head. "I thought it had all been an act."

"It wasn't an act," I say. "It was not my intention to gain the emperor's attention. It was Suyin's idea to make the prince a gift, and I couldn't think of a reason not to. I never thought it would lead to...to this." I motion to my headdress. "But once I started to gain the emperor's favor, what could I do? I would have been a fool to reject him."

"I suppose that is true," she says, looking back out at the girls. I pick up a long blade of grass and twirl it in my fingers. "Are you happy now?"

Her question surprises me, and I think it must show on

my face. She straightens up so she can look me in the face more easily.

"I mean, this isn't the life you wanted, but are you happy with how things have turned out?"

I have to think about this for a long moment. I haven't considered my own happiness for quite some time. I let go of that long ago. I have spent every day doing what is required of me whether it makes me happy or not. Have I somehow slipped into happiness without knowing it? No, I don't think I have. But there is something else. Something strangely comfortable.

"I am content," I say. "There are things I would change if I could, certainly. But that is not how the world works. If I have to live the rest of my life the way things are right now, I do not think I could complain in the end. Except about not seeing my family. That is a pain that never goes away."

Wangli turns the letter in her hand over. "Yes, that is a loss I would not wish upon anybody. Do you think I will be content one day?"

I reach out and rub her shoulder. "I can only hope that we will be content together." Wangli smiles and I hope that I have helped lighten her heart a bit. I stand up to go to the girls and hear a commotion down one of the garden paths. I walk toward the noise and see several ladies huddled together, all of them talking over each other.

"What is going on?" I ask. The crowd parts and everyone kneels. I can see that they were all circled around one woman who is holding a piece of paper. "What is that?"

"A letter from home, your majesty," the woman says, handing it to me. "From my mother."

I cannot read, but I take the paper anyway and hand it to Wangli. "What does it say?"

Wangli looks over the paper before answering. She

seems to hesitate. "It says that two of her brothers, her uncle, and a cousin have all been called to join the military."

The women all begin talking, fretting, and even crying.

"My brother was summoned too," another woman says.

"I heard that my whole village was ordered to serve," another says.

"The foreigners are destroying the coastal towns," another adds in.

They go on like this, sharing stories and gossip and some things that are surely wild tales. It has become impossible to keep the women in the dark regarding the war. Even here in the Forbidden City, we are not completely shielded from the outside world as long as even some of the women receive letters from home.

"That's enough," I say, clapping my hands. The ladies all go quiet and bow to me. "I have spoken to his majesty about this. He has assured me that there is nothing to fear."

"But...but the letters. My brothers..." the woman says, taking her letter back from Wangli and holding it tightly to her chest.

"I am sure it is true that they have been asked to join the army," I say. "But it is only to show the might of China to the foreigners. To frighten them into backing down."

"There has been fighting!" one of the other girls pipes up, and I groan inside. They seem to have far more information than I thought. "The foreigners have come onshore and been slaughtering villagers." The women all shriek and cry at this.

"Stop, stop!" I say. "Do you dare contradict the words of his majesty? Your husband?"

The girls go silent at this, though they still sniffle and tremor.

"I have spoken to him on the matter and you have no reason to fear. We are safe here in the Forbidden City, and his majesty will do all he can to protect this country."

They are quiet, but I can tell they are bursting to tell me more or ask questions.

"Please, majesty," one of the girls finally says. "Can you speak to the emperor on my behalf? If my brothers die, there will be no one to carry on the family line. My parents will be childless."

My heart goes out to her, but I know there is nothing that I can do. "I am sure your brothers will return home soon, safe and sound."

"But, your majesty..." All the girls begin pleading with me for help. To do something, anything, for their menfolk.

"I'm sorry," I try to say. I want to reassure them, but I do not want to make promises I cannot keep. I look to Wangli for assistance, but she shrugs. She has no idea what to do either.

"What is the meaning of this?" Dowager Empress Fenfeng says from behind me. I had not been able to hear her approach over the babbling of the ladies. Everyone drops to their knees.

"Good morning, Mother," they say.

"Why is everyone crying and yelling?" she asks. "I could hear the commotion all the way to my sitting room."

"The ladies have received letters from home telling them about the little conflict we are having with the foreigners. They are worried about their families," I say.

"Why would ladies of the court, the consorts of the emperor, worry themselves about such matters?" Fenfeng says harshly. "Your husband's family is the only family you need concern yourselves with now. Did your parents teach you nothing?"

The girls are silent.

"Now, the emperor has assured me that there is nothing to worry about. We are safe within these walls and that is all that matters. Do you all understand me?"

"Yes, Mother," they all say in unison.

"Good. Now, return to your palaces and speak no more of this. If I hear any more about it, you'll be locked in your rooms."

"Yes, Mother!" The women all stand and back away from Fenfeng before rushing back to their palaces. Fenfeng then turns to me, looking down her broad nose from her much taller pot-bottom shoes. I give a small bow.

"Thank you for your assistance, Mother," I say. "I tried to reassure them that there was nothing to worry about, but they are quite frightened."

"And why were they frightened?" she asks.

"Be...because of the letters—"

"No," she says. "It is because you allowed them to become frightened. The ladies should not be concerned about matters beyond these walls."

"What do you expect me to do?" I ask. "I cannot control what their families tell them."

"No," she says, "but you can keep them from seeing it."

"What do you mean? You can't expect me to...to keep the letters from them."

"If the letters contain information that could disrupt the harmony of the emperor's household, then that is exactly what you should do," she says.

"You...you want me to...to read their letters? To hide their letters?"

"There is no need for you to waste your time with such drudgery," she says. "Speak to Fiyanggu. Tell him that from now on, the department of household affairs is to read every letter that comes in. Any that mention a war, or fighting, or the military should be destroyed."

Wangli gasps and I see her shove her hands into her sleeves. She seems to be afraid Fenfeng will rip her letter away from her right now.

"That seems rather extreme," I say. "The ladies find great comfort in words from home."

"In normal times, yes, of course they do. But letters that speak of war are only causing them upset. They are full of supposition, lies, and tales that undermine the emperor. The only thing any of us need to know is the emperor's word on the matter."

I understand what Fenfeng is saying, and her words do align with what Guozhi told me. None of us wish to see the ladies of the harem in a panic. That would help no one. But in order to do that, the true situation must be kept from them.

"If you are not up to the task, I will speak to Fiyanggu myself," Fenfeng says.

"No," I say quickly. "I will do it. It is my responsibility. I will do as you ask."

"See that you do," she says as she turns and walks away. I see one of her maids hanging back, watching me, and I know Fenfeng will know if I fail to follow her orders.

"Please, majesty," Wangli says as we slowly walk toward Fiyanggu's office. "Please, do not do this. The letters from home are the only comfort many of us have."

"I'm not going to destroy the letters," I say. "But if I don't do something, Fenfeng will make sure they are done away with."

"What are you going to do?"

"I am going to order that the letters are only to be stored away for now," I say. "After the conflict is over, I will make sure the letters are delivered. The scary information the letters might hold will be outdated at that point and should not cause any problems."

"But...you are still going to order Fiyanggu to open the letters? To read them?" Wangli asks, concern etched on her brow.

"I don't see how I have a choice," I say with a shrug. "He will have to have some way to find out what the letters entail.

"Yes, of course." She looks sad, afraid.

"I...I guess I could make an exception for you and Yanmei, as my ladies," I say. She perks up at that.

"Really?"

"You must promise me that you will not tell anyone the content of the letters," I say. "If Fenfeng were to find out, she will go over my head and see for herself that future letters are destroyed."

"Thank you!" she says, hugging me.

I am still not happy about the situation. I hate the idea of violating the ladies' privacy. Of keeping information about their families from them, but I don't know what else to do right now. At least I am able to use my position to help my friends, even if it is just a little bit.

11

The weather is quite fine as spring turns to summer. The gardens of the inner court are blooming with flowers of every color. The grass is green and the trees are full. Many of the ladies have cats and small dogs as pets, and many of the animals have been giving birth to litters. The ladies all fawn over the cute little things, and everyone wants to keep them, but if that happens, we will soon be overrun with them.

"Most people just toss them in the river," Jinhai offers quite unhelpfully.

"That's disgusting," I say, stopping my embroidery to glower at him. He shrugs.

"There's no way to stop them from breeding. You can only get rid of the offspring."

"I've warned the ladies to keep their females pets from the males," I say.

"That clearly has not worked," Yanmei says. "Some of them make the most obnoxious racket if they are not allowed to roam at night."

"If they want pets, they need to be prepared for the

consequences," I say. "I don't want to ban pets altogether. I know many of the ladies love their pets like...like children almost. I don't want to take that from them."

"Animals have minds of their own," Jinhai goes on. "Even well-watched ones will manage to sneak away somehow."

I sigh. "I hate the idea of killing them, though. It's cruel. And it will upset the ladies greatly should they hear of it."

"Then what else can we do with them?" I ask.

"You could give them away as gifts," Huiyin says. Huiyin, one of the older concubines, has been coming to my palace regularly to visit and is becoming someone I would count as a friend.

"To whom?" I ask.

"To the wives and daughters of palace officials," she says. "My mother received several animal gifts over the years from Empress Fenfeng even though I don't think the two of them ever met. She received dogs, cats, birds, some of which she passed on to me and my sisters."

"Sounds like a lot of pets," I say. "Your home must have been overrun."

"No," she says. "It was never a problem."

I'm quiet for a moment, pondering how this was possible. I then realize that her mother must have ordered the offspring to...uh...be disposed of, as Jinhai had suggested.

"That's rather sad, isn't it?" I say.

"Once the animals leave the palace, they are not your concern," Huiyin says, patting my knee as if I am an upset child. "Besides, some find good homes. Mother still has several of her animals."

"I suppose you are right," I say. "I can't worry about what happens to them once they are no longer within my walls. Jinhai, make a list of women to who I can send gifts and make the arrangements to send the kittens and puppies away as soon as they are old enough."

"Yes, my lady," he says. He steps across the courtyard and speaks to another eunuch, who then trots off to do whatever Jinhai told him. There is actually very little Jinhai himself does anymore. He is my chief eunuch, and he has more eunuchs under him than I can count. Jinhai mainly stands within earshot, taking my orders and seeing them done. I have to admit, it is rather nice to make a request and see it done with no fuss. I've become quite spoiled.

"I heard that the emperor summoned you to his room three times in the last month," I say to Yanmei. She blushes as she concentrates on her embroidery. "I don't suppose there is any sign that you could be carrying the next emperor?"

She stops her work and her smile falters. "No, your majesty. Not that I am aware of."

"I am sure it is only a matter of time," I say. Yanmei does not look reassured by my words. Huiyin is quiet, focusing on her embroidery.

"I have put your name forward several times," I say to Huiyin. "I am sorry he has not summoned you."

"Next to Yanmei, he has been calling Lady Euhmeh to his bed the most," Wangli, who has been rather quiet all this time, says.

I don't know why this worries me, but it does. Euhmeh has been very cold to me ever since I assigned Lady Qiao to assist her. Euhmeh only speaks to me when I ask her a question directly, and even then, her answers are curt. I think the emperor gave me bad advice on that account. After all, he has no idea how things really are in the Inner Court.

Quite often, I have seen Euhmeh in the company of

Dowager Empress Fenfeng. She seems to have been made one of Fenfeng's ladies and was promoted to rank four. I have a feeling that Euhmeh has replaced Lady An in Fenfeng's affections, and I'm not sure how I feel about it. Despite Lady An's close relationship with Fenfeng, she fell victim to a terrible plot and lost her life. I'm still certain that Lady An was innocent, and that the person truly behind the assassination attempt is still out there. I'm not sure who is in the greater danger, me or Euhmeh.

"Well, I do hope someone falls pregnant soon," I say, shaking myself from my thoughts. "It would lighten his majesty's mood considerably."

"It would be wonderful to have more children in the palace," Yanmei says. "Especially a little prince."

The ladies begin to talk and giggle about children and how to spoil them while I sit quietly, enjoying the peace my life has found. I've nearly forgotten about the troubles with the foreigners and the threat of war. The emperor has not spoken to me about it again, and I'm beginning to think we packed up all those trunks in foolish haste. But then a eunuch announces that his majesty has arrived at my palace. All of us drop what we are doing and move to the main courtyard, where we bow in greeting. It is not until I stand up that I see Guozhi is wearing leather armor.

"What's happening?" I ask, my heart racing. I had gotten too comfortable. He is here to tell me I need to flee, I'm sure of it.

"I am riding out to meet with the foreigners," he says. "Their treaty terms are— Well, I will not burden you with the affairs of men. I only wanted to tell you that I will be gone for a few days, but that you are not to worry. I will return soon."

"Are you going...to...to fight?" I ask, my eyes roving over

the leather that smells and looks like new. The carved, five-toed dragon on the chest, even with its snarling teeth, does not give me confidence.

"No," he says. "I am riding out with a battalion as a show of force that I will not be intimidated into accepting unfair terms."

I nod. "That is good," I say, but I am lying. It is terrible. How could things have reached such a dangerous point? I have no idea, and I'm sure I never will. I am completely shut out of what is going on. I have no information and no way to help.

"I did not want you and the other ladies to worry about my absence," he says. "I shall return soon, I promise."

"I hope so," I say, and that, at least, is the truth. It is safer for the emperor, for all of us, if he stays within the great, red walls of the Forbidden City.

Guozhi takes my hand and kisses the back of it. I hold onto his hand tightly, willing him to stay. He looks down into my eyes and I am sure he sees fear there. I cannot read his expression. As the emperor, he has learned to mask his emotions, his feelings. He can never be too careful and let others discern his true feelings on matters. Most often, I have seen nothing more than a blank stare on his face than any look of love or affection. He reaches up and cups my cheek, giving me a reassuring smile. His mask cracks ever so slightly as he chuckles and then steps away from me.

"I will send word of my victory as soon as it is assured," he says. We all crouch down before him, the servants performing full kowtows.

"May the emperor live ten thousand years!" we all say.

The emperor turns and leaves the courtyard. As soon as he is over the threshold, I stand and go to the doorway, watching his retreating back. I hope that this is not the last time I ever see him.

I hear anxious voices behind me. When I turn around, the ladies are huddling together, comforting those that are crying. I see the servants rush out of the courtyard and know that they are off to tell the others what has happened. In a matter of minutes, the knowledge that the emperor has ridden off to war will fill the Forbidden City. The panic that the emperor wanted to avoid is about to rush through the palace like a torrent.

"Call an audience," I tell Jinhai. "Now. Every lady must attend."

"Yes, your majesty," he says. I have to try to get ahead of this, try to calm fears before they overrun the peaceful calm of my house. Why didn't Guozhi tell me this in private? Why did he have to come here, make a show of leaving? I shake my head. I cannot begin to understand him. Perhaps he was trying to make a show of strength to us too. To show us that he is not afraid, so we shouldn't be either. I don't know.

I must waste time changing into a better gown and having my hair styled. I usually undress after morning audiences and wear items that are a bit less ostentatious, but I must return to my formal appearance when calling an audience. My appearance is one of the only things that set me apart—and above—the other ladies of the harem.

As I leave, I see one of the eunuchs from the department of household affairs deliver a letter to Wangli. I try to ignore it, but I know Huiyin saw it as well. Any letter that doesn't mention the war is still delivered to the ladies, but those are few, a fraction of what usually arrives daily. Wangli is the only person still receiving all of her letters. I look the other way, but I am sure the other ladies will notice eventually, if they haven't already.

As I step out of the palace, I cannot even reach my sedan chair before I am swarmed with ladies. They surround me, faces all streaked with tears, voices mingled so I cannot understand them.

"I have called an audience where I will explain everything," I say, but I do not think they hear me. I try to speak louder. "Please, join the others in the audience hall—" One woman grabs my hand, nearly pulling me over while others fall at my feet. I look to Jinhai for help, and he tries to pull the ladies back, but he must be careful that he does not cause any of them offense. Most of them shrug him off and keep crying at me.

"Enough!"

The ladies instantly go quiet. I turn and see that Fenfeng has arrived. She had been in her sedan hair, being carried to the audience hall, but must have seen the commotion and stopped and climbed out to get the situation under control. I wish I could be more grateful, but I know she is going to use the incident to undermine me.

"Empress Lihua has called a formal audience," Fenfeng says harshly. "Go, all of you. Now!"

"Yes, Mother."

"Of course, Mother."

"Right away, Mother."

The ladies make their apologies and compose themselves as they back away from us and return to their own palaces to make themselves presentable.

"Thank you, Mother," I say. "The ladies must be forgiven for being afraid."

"They must not!" she says. "Dignity, Lihua. In all matters, we must retain our dignity."

I flash back to a time when Mingxia said the same thing to me during my training, when I was living in her home. *Your dignity is the most important aspect of your character and bearing,* she told me. *Maintain your dignity above all things.*

"During trying times," Fenfeng goes on, "if we cannot maintain our dignity, then we have nothing."

"Yes, Mother," I say, giving a bow. "I am sure the ladies were just in shock. They will surely collect themselves now."

Fenfeng takes a step closer to me, looking down her nose. "The emperor, my *son*, is no longer here to help you. If you cannot manage the harem on your own in his absence, *someone* will have to step in."

I do my best not to snort a laugh. The emperor has been gone less than an hour, and already she is trying to usurp my place as empress. I look up at her and give my sweetest smile.

"If I need help, the emperor has many *wives* I can call upon for assistance."

Fenfeng scoffs. "The harem is already in chaos. When the emperor returns, he will learn just how unsuited to your position you are."

"I will always rejoice in the emperor's return," I say, "no matter what his opinion of me may be."

She presses her lips into a thin line, clearly angry that the barbs she throws at me have no effect. If I were demoted from empress—if such a thing were possible—I would be glad of it. I will not fail in my duties intentionally. I would not want to cause the emperor such distress. But should I do my best and he still find me wanting, I will accept my fate with as much dignity as I can muster. But I would not mourn losing my position if such a thing should happen.

Fenfeng turns away from me and climbs back into her sedan chair with the help of a eunuch.

I breathe a sigh of relief, but I know the relief will be short-lived. I now must face over a hundred frightened ladies and somehow lead them through this crisis.

12

Allaying the women's fears seems to become my only job over the following days. They come to my palace at all hours, even during the night. I try to tell them that everything will be all right, but they know something is terribly wrong.

The longer the emperor is away from the Forbidden City, the more afraid the women grow. Rumors that the emperor has been taken captive, or even killed, are rife. They also notice when they stop receiving letters from home, which only makes them more afraid. They fear the worst for their families, that they have been killed in the fighting somewhere, and that is the reason why they have stopped writing. All I can do is pat their hands, hug them, and repeat the same words over and over again: everything is fine.

It's a lie I repeat so often throughout the day, it has lost all meaning. I wish I could say the words enough to convince myself they are true, but that is impossible. The emperor has been gone for days and I have received no updates. I do not believe he is dead. If he were, we certainly would be told that there was a new emperor. That Prince Honghui is now emperor. But has the emperor been captured? Have the negotiations gone sour? Is there increased fighting and casualties? Or have things calmed and settled and the emperor and foreigners are celebrating together? I don't know.

As much as possible, I offer distractions for the inner court. I have an opera troupe put on performances from morning until late at night. I invite large groups of ladies to dine with me or take tea. I send them all bolts of silk and bobbins of thread so they can make new clothes. I send art supplies to the women who enjoy painting and new instruments to those with musical talents. It helps, but only a little.

I keep the children in a smaller courtyard in the back of my palace so they will not be disturbed by the women visiting me in the front courtyard. Jiangfei seems to take no notice of the tension around her, innocent thing she is. But Dongmei seems to sense every change in the air. She is always tense, never smiles, and hardly plays with her sister. She mostly sits by the pond, watching the fish and petting the dogs or cats that sit by her side. I try to reassure her as I do the others, but Dongmei will not be consoled. Of all the girls in the palace, I think she may be the most clever, which is usually a good thing. But now, it causes her no small amount of anxiety, and I feel powerless to relieve it.

I am in the courtyard, speaking to a few women who have come to me for comfort, when I realize that I have not seen Wangli all day. And I'm not sure I saw her the day before either. I ask Jinhai to find out if she is ill and think little else of it. I'm sure she only has a stomachache and wishes to stay in bed. If it is more serious than that, I will send for the doctor.

Sometime later, Jinhai returns, his face grave.

"What is it?" I ask.

He takes my elbow and turns me aside so he can whisper in my ear without the other ladies hearing. "I think you need to come with me," he says.

"Why?" I ask, suddenly worried for my friend's health. "Is Wangli terribly ill?"

"No," he says.

"Then what is the matter?"

He hesitates, looking around at the courtyard full of women. "You need to come with me, my lady," he whispers again.

My mind is racing, jumping to the worst possible conclusions. Is she dead? Has she...perhaps died by her own hand? Was she injured, or even killed, by someone else?

I order the visitors out of my palace, and Jinhai, Yanmei, and Suyin escort me to my sedan chair. I am nearly sick with worry by the time we arrive at Wangli's palace, which is not far away.

As soon as I step out, I hear a commotion. Yelling and crying. When I step through the gate into the courtyard, I am horrified to see a senior eunuch from the ministry of household affairs whipping one of Wangli's maids. The rest of Wangli's staff is lined up, forced to watch the terrible torture.

"I don't know!" she is crying as he whips her again and again.

"How can you not know?" he yells down at her.

"Stop this!" I order. The eunuch immediately does as I command, and everyone in the courtyard kowtows to me. I turn to Jinhai. "Now, what is going on? Where is Wangli?"

"We do not know, your majesty," Jinhai says.

I have to blink because I am not immediately sure I heard him right. "What? What do you mean?"

"According to her servants, when they woke up yesterday morning, she was gone."

"Gone? Yesterday?" I gasp. "She's been gone more than a day? Why was I not told? Where is her eunuch?"

A thin, young man with a shaved head crawls forward, his body trembling. "I am Lady Wangli's chief eunuch."

"Sit up so I can hear you," I say. "Tell me everything you know."

He sits back on his heels and keeps his face turned to the ground. Still, his voice is low and shaking so hard, I have to strain to hear him.

"Yesterday morning, when the maid who sleeps at the foot of her bed awoke, she saw that Lady Wangli was not in her bed." He looks at the maid, who is now covered in red lashes. "Sometimes, the lady wakes up early and walks in the garden. But this time, we could not find her.

"We searched everywhere, the whole palace, and the grounds around her palace. Every pond, every well, every pavilion. We could find her nowhere."

I nod and turn to Jinhai. "Organize a search. I want the entire inner court explored. Every single room in every single palace, understand?"

"Yes, my lady."

I turn back to Wangli's eunuch. "Then what? When you could not find your lady, why did you not tell me?" All of the servants start to cry again.

"We were afraid, your majesty," the boy says.

I press my lips and turn away in frustration. They had to know that they could not keep her disappearance a secret for long. We may have lost precious time in finding Wangli.

"You are not responsible for the actions of your lady," I

say, looking over the cowering servants. "If any of you were involved in her disappearance, you will, of course, be punished. But right now, finding Wangli is of utmost importance."

"Yes, your majesty," they all say.

"Fiyanggu is leading the search, my lady," Jinhai tells me. I nod, but I have a sinking feeling in my stomach.

Where could she be? If she were anywhere in the inner court, surely she would have been found by now. Of course, if she came to a bad end, her body might be hidden somewhere. I hate to think of it, but it will be better to know the truth than continue worrying. But if she is nowhere in the inner court, then she must have, somehow, left the Forbidden City.

I feel a bit dizzy remembering the one time I snuck out of the Forbidden City. I had not been a concubine long and desperately missed my family. I stole a maid's clothes, climbed a tree, and fell to the ground outside the palace wall. It was stupid, dangerous, especially since I did not have a plan for getting back into the Forbidden City, fool that I was. If Honghui hadn't found me, hadn't let me back in, I shudder to think of what would have happened to me. Of what will happen to Wangli now.

"Send word to Wangli's family," I say. "Perhaps she is there."

Jinhai seems confused for a moment. "You think she left the Forbidden City?"

"I don't know," I say. "But anything is possible right now. Maybe she missed them or was worried about them."

Jinhai hesitates and then speaks to me in a low voice. "My lady, if Wangli left the Forbidden City...the punishment will be great."

"I know," I whisper back. "But what else can I do?"

He nods and then goes to one of his eunuchs to issue the order. I turn back to Wangli's servants.

"So, when you found your mistress was missing, you stayed silent on the matter because you were afraid of being punished. Have you done anything to try and find out what happened to her? Where she might have gone?"

"Yes, your majesty," her chief eunuch says. "We found that a large amount of cash and jewels are missing."

I feel sick at his words and put my hand to my mouth. So, she most certainly left the Forbidden City, and she took her money and jewels with her.

"Where did she go?" I ask them. They are all silent, but a few exchange glances. I want to yell and scream at them, force them to tell me. But I see the red welts on the maid and know that yelling at people who are already afraid will not convince them to talk. I clear my throat and take a calming breath.

"As I said, I will not punish you for the actions of your lady. I only want to find her and make sure she is safe. I am certain that she did not tell you about her plan. But you must know something. Did she say something in the past that seemed innocent at the time but is now suspicious? Was she acting strangely?"

"One of my uniforms is missing," the maid who was beaten says. I can see the eunuch who was whipping her grew angry. Apparently, I was able to get information out of the maid that he was not.

"Get out," I tell the eunuch. His eyes go wide and he kowtows before crawling out of the courtyard. I turn to Jinhai. "I don't want him anywhere near Wangli's servants."

"Yes, my lady."

"So, she is dressed as a maid," I say. "She undoubtedly did not want to look like a runaway from the imperial city.

She wanted to blend in." I know this because it is what I would do. What I *did* do when I ran away. I keep that to myself, of course.

"She has almost certainly left the Forbidden City," I say out loud, though to no one in particular. "Then where did she go? To her parents? Why? If she is found there, they will certainly be held accountable."

The servants are silent for a moment, and I think it is because they don't have anything to add. But apparently, it is just her eunuch getting up his courage to speak.

"I do not think she is with her parents, your majesty."

"Why do you think that?"

He reaches into his sleeve and pulls out a charred piece of paper. "We discovered that she burned most of her letters in a brazier. But part of this one survived."

He hands it to me. I can't read it, of course, so I don't know if there is anything useful on the paper. I give it to Jinhai.

"What does it say?"

Jinhai examines the paper, squinting to read the characters. "It is not much, my lady. But it seems to be a signature. It says something to the effect of, 'your dearest love, Jun.'"

All the air rushes out of my lungs and I fear I will faint. Suyin rushes up to me, taking one of my hands. She leads me to a stone bench where I can sit down. I rub my forehead.

She has a lover.

Suddenly, everything makes sense. Why she was crying the night we met. Why she didn't want to be called to the emperor's bed. Why she was afraid of her letters being opened. I then feel sick.

This is partly my fault.

She was still receiving letters. I thought they were from

her family. She *told me* they were from her family. But that was a lie. They were from her lover, but I couldn't know that because I can't read. I shake my head, trying to order my thoughts.

Was her lover recruited for the military? She had told me that her brother had been. Was that a complete lie? Or was she really talking about her lover? Is that why she ran away? Did they both run away together? They must be together. They clearly love each other. Why they decided to run away *now*, though, I cannot truly know.

What I do know is that I hope Wangli and her lover are never found. If they are, they will both be put to death. Even though she has broken the law and her marriage to the emperor, I sympathize with her. Have I not been in her shoes? Have I not done the same, and worse? The Forbidden City is a cold and lonely place. For some women, to be forced to give your body to a man you did not choose, it is torture. For me, it is merely a duty. But I did not know love before I came here. If I'd had a lover on the outside, there was a time when I'm sure I would have risked all to be with him. I *have* risked everything, once upon a time.

I hope Wangli escapes, and that she and her lover are happy together. But I cannot say such words out loud. I can never appear to be approving of such behavior.

"Jinhai," I finally say. "Alert the palace guards and the city watch. Send men to her family's home. Do whatever you can to find her."

"Yes, your majesty," he says.

I stand and return to Wangli's servants. "You are all dismissed. You may either report for reassignment or you may return to your families."

There is a great sigh of relief all around, and then tears of joy. They all crawl to me, kissing the hem of my robe and uttering their thanks. I turn to leave and see Yanmei, her own face red and swollen. I had forgotten she was here. She and Wangli had grown quite close over the last few months. I go to her and take her in my arms.

"It will be all right," I say. And this time, I believe it is true. If Wangli is smart—and I know she is—she is already far away from the Forbidden City and will never be found.

"We will never see her again, will we?" Yanmei says. I shake my head. "No. She is either lost to us forever, or..." I don't want to speak the alternative if she is found.

Yanmei nods. There is more she wants to say, I can feel it. I believe she is secretly hoping that Wangli has gotten away safely, but she would never say it out loud either. I look into her eyes and nod, hoping that she can see in my expression that I feel the same way. She hugs me again, but it feels a little less sad this time.

"Come," I say. "We must tell the others."

"Must we?" Yanmei asks, her face alarmed. "Everyone will gossip about it endlessly."

"That is what I am hoping," I say. "Let them talk about something other than a possible war with the foreigners for at least one day."

Maybe at least a small amount of good will come from Wangli's escape if I can get a moment's peace.

13

The ground beneath our feet shakes so violently, items fall from shelves and one of my ladies is knocked off balance from her pot-bottom shoes. Then, all is silent, save the pounding in my ears from my racing heart. Even the birds, which had been singing just a moment ago, are quiet.

"What was that, Lihua?" Dongmei asks me, her eyes wide as she pulls her little sister closer to her.

"I don't know," I say. I look up at the sky, which is such a perfectly clear blue, there is not a single cloud in the sky. Then, the ground shakes again, and this time I hear a rumble in the distance. From beyond the golden tops of the building in the Forbidden City, a column of black smoke rises.

The worst has happened. War has come, and it is time to flee.

"Everyone," I say, "back to your palaces. Close the doors and await further instruction."

Some of the women run from my courtyard, others are

paralyzed by fear and must be escorted out by maids and eunuchs. Yanmei looks at me with large, pleading eyes.

"Not you," I say. "You are to stay with me and the girls."

"What is happening?" she asks. "I thought... You said everything was fine."

There is no need to keep Yanmei in the dark any longer. "It was my responsibility to keep the women calm."

Her hand flies to her mouth. "What is happening? What are we to do?"

I look to Jinhai. "Ready the carts." He gives a quick bow and then runs off. I then turn to Suyin. "Bring the trunks to the gate."

"The trunks?" Yanmei asks.

"We might still be safe here in the Forbidden City," I tell her. "But if the fighting is that close, I believe we may have to flee."

"Flee? Flee where? What fighting?"

I shake my head. I don't have time to explain everything right now. "Do not worry. I have taken care of everything. Sit here with the girls for now. Send your servants to your palace to retrieve your cash and jewels. You need nothing else. I have packed enough supplies for you and—"

I was about to say "you and Wangli," but then I remember that Wangli is gone. In the days since her disappearance was discovered, she still has not been found. Wherever she is, I hope she is safe.

"I've packed enough supplies for you," I say. "When the time comes, I will tell you what to do."

She nods and then drops down onto a stone stool, pulling the girls into her arms.

"I'm scared, Lihua," Dongmei says. I try to give her a reassuring smile.

"Don't be," I say. "All will be well. I promise."

I go to my dressing room and remove the tall headdress from my head. I leave my hair tied up, though, so it stays out of the way. I exchange my pot-bottom shoes for flat slippers and change into a plainer robe. I hide a small bag of coins and jewels in one of my sleeve pockets. By the time Suyin returns from moving the trunks, I am ready to leave.

Back in the courtyard, I see that Jinhai has returned with three donkey carts and parked them just outside the gate. He orders the other eunuchs to load the trunks onto two of the carts. The other one will be for me, the girls, and Yanmei. The servants will all have to walk alongside the carts. We don't climb into the carts immediately, though. It may be that we are still perfectly safe within the Forbidden City. The foreigners might attack the city, but leave the palace intact. All we can do is wait.

The ground shakes with more frequency, the roaring growing ever closer. I see a sedan chair being carried toward us. It is the dowager empress. Unlike the other ladies, I cannot order her to stay in her palace. She is helped from the chair and then stalks toward me, her face furious. She looks at the laden carts.

"So, you are prepared to leave," she says. "When my servants told me you were loading donkey carts with your necessary items, I hardly believed it."

"I was told that I should prepare myself and my household should we need to leave. Discretion was required to avoid a panic. I had assumed that you were told the same thing." A lie, of course. In truth, I had not given a single thought to what would happen to Fenfeng should I need to flee. And it seems that Honghui didn't either.

"I was sworn to secrecy," I say, "in order to keep the harem calm."

"This is ridiculous," she says. "You are doing the exact

opposite. The walls of the Forbidden City will not be breached."

There is the sound of a loud explosion and the ground shakes again. Fenfeng's face blanches as she holds tightly to her eunuch's hand to keep from falling.

"I pray that you are right, Mother," I say when the rumbling stops. "But I cannot take any chances, and neither should you. You should prepare yourself should the worst happen."

"I will do no such thing!" she says as if I greatly insulted her. "I have lived in this palace for over forty years and will not be chased from my home by a bunch of foreign animals."

She stares at me, waiting for some sort of reply. What does she want me to say? Does she want me to beg her to come with us? I say nothing. I care not whether she tries to flee with us or stays here.

After a moment, she turns and climbs back into her sedan chair. I do wonder what will happen when the emperor finds out I made no preparations for his mother to leave. People are supposed to always put their parents first. But since the emperor himself did not tell me to prepare to flee, I will have to plead ignorance on the matter.

I do not know how long we wait, lined up against the wall of my palace in the sun, listening to explosions, rumblings, and eventually gunshots. The fighting is getting closer by the minute. How long are we to wait for instructions?

"Jinhai," I say. "If we were to leave, do you know the way to Jehol? To the Winter Palace?"

"I have not been there, majesty," he says. "But the road north out of Peking is well-traveled. It should not be difficult to find our way to the fort."

I nod but do not give the order to leave. I am torn. If we are safe here, of course I would prefer to stay. But if we must flee, I do not want to wait until it is too late. Until our enemies block our way.

Suddenly, dozens of eunuchs run into the inner court, Fiyanggu at the head of them. He runs to me and kneels.

"Get up! There is no time for that!" I tell him.

"Majesty," he says, out of breath, "the foreigners are coming. They are marching through Peking right now."

"I've been listening to their approach all morning," I growl at him. "What are we to do."

"Flee, your majesty."

For a moment, my vision goes black. I thought I had prepared for this, expected it. But actually hearing the words stabs my heart with ice and terror runs through my veins. I shake the sensation off quickly. There is no time to be afraid.

"Everyone," Fiyanggu says.

"Everyone?" I ask.

"Everyone. His majesty sent orders that everyone in the Forbidden City, especially all the ladies, are to go to Jehol."

My mouth goes dry. "Were the orders for you?" I ask, my voice cracking. "Or for me?"

"For you, your majesty."

The ground beneath me seems to open up and I can feel myself falling, falling. My mind spins and I feel sick.

"My lady!" Yanmei says, grasping my arm. "What does this mean? What are we to do?"

I'm suddenly so angry. How dare Guozhi task me with such an order with no warning? I am now to gather over a hundred palace ladies together and usher them to safety myself? Not to mention the countless servants.

And the empress dowager.

But I must do so. It is an order from the emperor. If he were to find out I fled, alone, with only those closest to me, and left everyone else behind after I learned of his orders, he would be furious. He would hold me responsible for their fates.

"Majesty," Jinhai says. "What are we to do?"

His voice reminds me that I have no time to dally. I must get as many people out of the Forbidden City as soon as possible. I turn to Yanmei.

"Yanmei, take the girls, take my carts, take my servants and yours, and go, now."

"Without you?" she asks.

"I must stay, must evacuate the others. I will come as soon as I can."

Dongmei and Jinagfei begin to cry. "I'm scared!" Jiangfei says.

"Don't leave us!" Dongmei says. I kneel down in front of them.

"Listen, my darlings, I need you to be brave. You must be strong. Auntie Yanmei will take care of you. Obey her every word, understand?" The girls nod as they use their long, silk sleeves to wipe their faces. "I will be right behind you. I promise."

I stand back up and help Yanmei and the girls onto the donkey cart. These are not the typical donkey carts ladies use for traveling with silk pillows and canopies to block the sun. These carts are practical and open to the elements. Carts used for transporting goods, not people. I hope there is no bad weather on the journey.

"Don't stop for anyone or anything," I tell Yanmei as I hold her hand tight. "Go straight to Jehol."

"Yes, majesty," she cries. I don't want to let her hand go, but eventually I do. I turn to Jinhai and Suyin.

"You must go with them."

"No!" they both say, stepping close around me.

"We cannot leave you," Jinhai says.

"You will need our help," Suyin says. I shake my head and nudge them away from me.

"You are the only people who prepared for this. The children need you more than I do. And if you stay, that will be two more people for me to worry about. Please, I beg you, go!"

They hesitate, looking at each other, unsure of what to do.

"I am *ordering* you," I tell them, "as your empress."

Suyin bursts into tears and Jinhai bows.

"Yes, your majesty," he says.

The next explosion is so loud, I can hear it echo in my ears. Everyone ducks down, covering their ears as the ground shakes. The children scream.

"Go! Now!" I tell everyone when the sound clears. Jinhai grasps the donkey's bridle and urges the beast forward. Suyin runs along beside it. The girls turn around in their seat and watch me until the cart turns a corner, heading toward the east gate and out of the Forbidden City.

I am alone.

I take a deep breath to calm my racing heart and decide what to do first.

"Your majesty?" Fiyanggu says.

"Order the rest of the donkey carts to come here," I say. "They should line up in front of my palace."

"Yes, your majesty."

"Then send word to every palace lady. They are to pack a single bag with only the smallest and most necessary items. They are to wear flat shoes and come here as quickly as possible. We will put as many ladies as possible on each cart and send them on their way."

"Yes, your majesty," he says. He turns to his assistants and starts issuing orders, but not quickly enough for me. I will have to begin issuing the orders myself—starting with the empress dowager.

14

I don't get far before I am stopped by two ladies. They fall at my feet, their faces streaked with tears. Their maids are right behind them, trying to pull them away, but they wrench their arms from the girls' grasps.

"Majesty, what are we to do?" one asks.

"Help us! Please don't leave me!" the other says.

I bend down and take one of each of their arms and tug them to standing. "You do not need to be afraid. We are leaving—all of us, together."

"Where are we going?" one asks.

"It doesn't matter. Go back to your palaces and pack a bag, only one! Pack only necessities and then go to my palace. There will be carts waiting for you." I nod to the maids, and they once again work on pulling the ladies away from me.

"Wait! Your majesty—"

I ignore their calls and continue on my way to the empress dowager's palace. I cannot waste time on people who will not listen. The foreign armies are coming. I do not know how much time I have left.

I step through the gate into the courtyard of Fenfeng's palace. I am surprised to find nearly all of her household standing around idle! They look afraid, worried, huddled together in small groups, talking animatedly or crying. But that is all they are doing. None of them seem to understand the urgency of the situation. When they see me, they all drop to their knees.

"Get up," I tell them. "Pack a single bag each and prepare to leave." They all remain on their knees, looking dumbly from me to each other. "Have you no ears? Do as I say!"

"But...the dowager—" one of the maids starts to say.

"You dare question me?" I nearly scream.

The maid cowers to the ground. "No, your majesty! Never!"

"Then do as I say!"

The girl scrambles to her feet and out of the courtyard.

"All of you!" I yell. Everyone bows to me one more time, begging my forgiveness before disappearing.

"How dare you issue commands to my household!" Fenfeng says, coming out of her private chambers and into the courtyard. "You are not in charge here."

I don't waste time explaining to her that, as the empress and head of the harem, it *is* within my right to order her servants about.

"We must go, now," I tell her.

"What? I told you I will not leave."

"The *emperor* has ordered all of us to leave. To take the northern road to Jehol and the Winter Palace. The foreigners are advancing through the city and will be at the palace soon."

The empress's jaw drops and she stammers for words. I can tell that she is at once torn between defying me and obeying her son. Suddenly, there is a blast so close and so strong, that as the ground shakes, some loose roof tiles crash to the floor of the courtyard. One eunuch barely misses being smashed on the head. That seems to help Fenfeng make her decision.

"If my son commands it, then we will go," she says.

"Good," I say. "Have your servants each pack a single bag and then gather at my palace. A donkey cart will be waiting for you."

She looks at me as if she is about to argue, I assume about how much baggage she is allowed to take, but I do not stay to listen. I leave the palace and run to the next one, and then the next, issuing the same orders as I did to Fenfeng. I care not about rank or status in this moment, only about getting the women out and heading north as quickly as possible. If any ladies or maids or eunuchs get in my way, asking questions, I do not stop to answer them, but order them back to their homes.

I am near the west wall when I hear screams and gunshots coming from the other side. My heart sinks. The foreigners have already arrived and are outside our very gates! I feel sick as I think about the ladies exiting through the east wall. Are they getting away safely? Or am I sending them right into the arms of the enemy?

I run to the other side of the Forbidden City, which takes far too long, as large as the palace is. I am winded when I reach the other side and put my hands on my knees as I try to catch my breath. I see a cart carrying two ladies and two trunks ambling through the gate. The poor donkey pulling them seems to already be straining, but I can do nothing about that now. If we get far enough away from the city and it is safe to stop, I can perhaps order the women to unpack anything they don't need to lighten the load.

I go through the gate behind them, to the road that rings the Forbidden City. Down the road, toward the front of the palace, I see the backs of dozens of palace guards, though they are obscured by thick dust and smoke in the air. The guards are shouting and grunting, swinging swords above them. I cannot see the enemy through the crush of our soldiers, but I can hear words being shouted that I cannot understand. The sharp smell of blood is in the air, and I can hear gunshots and hear the screams of the dying.

Our soldiers appear to be holding back the foreigners, giving the women time to escape. But I do not know how long our men will last. I'm about to return through the wall when Honghui appears from the skirmish. I had seen him behind the guards, yelling orders, but I didn't realize it was him until he turned around. He runs to me and we clasp arms.

Honghui's face is covered with dust, streaked by sweat. There is a spray of blood on his right shoulder, with a few droplets on his neck. His queue has become untied and his plait is falling loose.

"Why are you still here?" he yells at me over the tumult around us.

"I have to get all the women out."

"You must get yourself out! Get out of here!"

"Guozhi ordered me to make sure all the women escape. I cannot leave them."

There is an explosion and Honghui pulls me to him protectively as the ground shakes under our feet.

"Where is the emperor?" I ask.

He hesitates for a moment. "He is already on the road to Jehol."

My stomach sinks. *He left us.* He left me! How could he?

I shake my head, trying to be rational. He is the emperor. He must live. If he were to be captured or killed, the war would be ended and then all of us would be at the mercy of the foreign devils.

I know that seeing to the emperor's safety first is most important. But still, the knowledge that the emperor—my supposed husband—has left us behind fills me with hurt and rage. I am ashamed of myself for preparing to leave the women behind. I never should have kept the need for preparations from them. I had assumed that the emperor would have a plan in place to evacuate the other women, but I had been wrong. I'd been foolish. I should have known that if the worst happened, the emperor would be the first to leave and the rest of us would be on our own.

"Take the next donkey cart available and get out of here!" Honghui yells. He starts to turn away, as if his word is the final say on the matter. But I hold fast to his arms.

"No," I say. "I will be on the last one, only after all the other women are safe."

"Dammit, Lihua!" Honghui says. "Do you not understand what is happening?"

"I'll not leave the wives of the emperor behind to be raped and slaughtered by foreign pigs."

His eyes go wide and his mouth gapes. That seems to finally have gotten through to him.

"Fine. But hurry. I do not know how long I can hold them back."

I nod and turn away, my hands slipping from his. As I reach the gate, I look back toward the fighting and can no longer see him.

I run back to my palace and pass several more donkey carts carrying ladies and goods. I stop when I meet a cart that has no ladies, but only several trunks. I stop the eunuch that is leading the donkey.

"What is this? Why are there no ladies with you?"

"They would have made the cart too heavy for the donkey to pull," he says.

I cannot believe that some of the ladies are putting their things ahead of their own lives. I grab the donkey's reins from him and lead it from the line. "Empty this cart right now and return for the women. The women are the priority."

The eunuch looks at me with wide eyes, his face going pale. "But...but, majesty, these are the empress dowager's things. She will beat me..."

I look past him to the line of carts and see three more carrying only trunks. I nearly scream in frustration.

"Empty this cart and return for the women now or I'll kill you myself!" I hate to say such a thing, but it is within my right to punish or even put to death any servant in the Forbidden City who has committed a serious enough offense against me.

The eunuch bows and starts to unload the cart. I give the same orders to the eunuchs pulling the other carts. When I reach the gate of my palace, there are still dozens of women waiting for a cart, and all of them are crying. At the head of the line is Fenfeng, countless trunks and bags piled up beside her, and more are being brought by the minute.

"What are you doing?" I scream at her. "These carts are for the women."

"I need the carts for my things. I cannot travel without my clothes, my headdresses—"

"Yes, you can," I tell her. "All of this is to be left behind." I turn to the eunuchs loading the trunks onto the cart.

"Unload it, now!" I step in front of a eunuch who was in the middle of loading another trunk onto the cart.

"How dare you!" Fenfeng says. "I am the empress dowager! I am the mother of the emperor. I am *your* mother. My word is law, and I say that none of my things can be left behind. Now, get out of my way."

"I am the empress!" I yell, stomping my foot. For the first time, I will use the full power and authority of my rank to do what needs to be done. "You will do as I say."

Fenfeng glares at me. "Never." She turns back to her servants. "Keep loading the carts or you will feel the board to your back until you are dead!"

"I'm warning you," I tell her, gritting my teeth. "Stop this or face the consequences."

At this, Fenfeng laughs. "You can't hurt me, stupid girl."

"I wasn't planning to," I say. I push past her into my palace and look around for anything useful. I go to the koi pond and pull up several cattails. I then go to the kitchen and the cooking fire that is always burning. I set the ends of the cattails alight, then I run back out of the palace.

The ladies who see me carrying the makeshift torch cry out. Fenfeng turns to me, her eyes wide with terror.

"Don't—!" she tries to yell, but I don't give her a chance to argue. I toss the cattails onto the stack of trunks and bags. Quickly, some of the bags catch fire.

The empress dowager lets out a scream as if she herself is in pain. "No! Stop it!"

I step between her and the growing bonfire. "Get on that donkey cart and get out of here or I will burn your whole palace down!" It is no idle threat, and I breathe hard as I stare her down.

The empress dowager bursts into tears and her ladies go to her side. Her tears have no effect on me.

"You are going to regret this, Lihua," she says as she turns toward the donkey cart. Her servants help her climb up and then lead the cart away. I breathe a small sigh of relief. The evacuation has been much delayed, but at least it can continue.

The carts, including those I had ordered emptied earlier, continue moving down the line, picking up the ladies and their modest goods. Finally, the last cart arrives, but there are still three ladies left, and myself.

"This is the last cart, majesty," Fiyanggu says. "You must get on it."

The three remaining ladies burst into tears. "Please don't leave us!" they beg.

"You are certain that there are no more left?" I ask Fiyanggu.

"I'm certain," he says. "We gathered every one we could find. Please, majesty, get on the cart."

My heart is racing. I told Honghui that I would be on the last cart. But I didn't account for the possibility that there wouldn't be enough for all of us. I remember what Honghui said, that my life was the most important in all the harem. That if I were captured, we could lose the war.

But then I remember Empress Caihong. I held her hand as she laid dying. *I have done my duty*, she told me as the baby was cut from her womb and the life drained out of her. She died doing what was expected of her. I can expect no less from myself.

"No," I say. "The emperor commanded me to save the ladies, and I will do my duty." The women stop crying and look at one another.

"No, majesty," one of them says. "Take my place."

"No, take mine," another says.

"We will not leave you," the other one says.

I feel guilty that I do not know the girls' names, though I have seen them plenty of times, yet they are willing to give up their places for me.

"No," I tell them. "I will be fine. I will walk along behind you if I must." They offer pitiful objections as I push them toward the cart, but I insist. Once they are all situated, I turn to Fiyanggu.

"Go with them, lead their cart."

"Majesty?"

"I will need you in Jehol," I say. "They will need you. The emperor will need you." In truth, I've never given Fiyanggu and his position much thought. But it was he who rounded up the carts, had the ladies brought together. I realize that much of the inner court runs smoothly thanks to him. I do not know how the harem would be able to function without him.

Fiyanggu hesitates, but then he bows. "Your Majesty." He takes off at a jog, leading the donkey and its cart out of the Forbidden City as quickly as possible.

When they exit the gate, I take one final look around to make sure we are leaving no one behind. That no one is arriving at the last minute. The inner court, once a place of beauty and wonder, is now full of smoke and dust. It is just as colorless as I remember the rest of Peking being when I lived beyond the red walls.

When I am satisfied that everyone has escaped, I turn to follow the last cart out of the Forbidden City. But, there is a loud crash behind me, followed by the yell of countless voices.

From the gate leading to the outer court, a dozen men in blue and red uniforms spill out. Their skin is pale white, but their lower faces are covered with hair. They are waving swords and guns as they spread out and run down the various pathways. I turn to run toward the east gate, but I don't get far.

Someone grabs me from behind and I stumble forward. I don't fall because he has a rough grip on my hair. I twist around and see the wild face of one of the pale foreigners. He grips both of my arms so I can't get away. He laughs and sticks out his tongue at me, his breath reeking and his teeth yellow. He says something in his strange, barking language. I twist my arms, trying to get away, but he's too strong for me. He tries to drag me along, but I dig my heels into the ground.

I hear the whinny of a horse and see the foreigner look up at something behind me. He releases my arms and I whirl around to see Honghui on the back of a large, brown horse. Honghui points a gun at the man and shoots him in the chest without a moment's hesitation. He then shoves the gun into his waistband and offers his hand to me. I take it and scramble up the side of the horse as he pulls me. I squeeze into the saddle behind him, wrapping my arms around his waist. I see more foreigners running toward us, waving their swords and pointing guns. Honghui turns the horse around and we ride to the gate. We both wince and duck as we hear the gunshots behind us, but neither we nor the horse are injured.

We ride through the gate and take the road north, leaving the Forbidden City in our wake. I do not look back.

15

____

s Honghui leads his horse around the tall, red walls of the Forbidden City, we quickly catch up to the caravan of donkey carts carrying the ladies. We have not gotten far, and seem to still be within Peking. I twist in the saddle to look back, expecting to see the foreigners chasing us. Instead, I only see throngs of local people, carrying bags and children, leading animals, and pushing wheelbarrows, trying to get away from the invaders with as many of their possessions as possible.

"Will the foreigners follow us?" I ask Honghui. "The donkey carts will not be able to out-run them. I can't believe we weren't told to leave until the invaders were at our very gates."

"No, they won't follow us," he says. "By taking over the Forbidden City, the throne, they have no need for more. They don't want to sack the city, only make their point to Guozhi."

The horse whinnies and side-steps to avoid stepping on someone. I hold tightly to Honghui to keep from falling off. There's not really enough room in the saddle for two people, but we have to make do. Honghui pulls the horse to the right, forcing it through the crowd to stay right behind the last cart.

"I'm sorry I didn't send word to you sooner," he says, his tone small and even, as though he is truly regretful, but the words are hard to say.

"I'm sure you did the best you could," I say, a lump in my throat. "If you hadn't told me weeks ago that this was a possibility, we probably would not have made it out. I would have been at a complete loss as to what to do."

"I'm sure my brother will be pleased with you," he says, and then he chuckles. "I'm actually surprised you managed to get everyone out. You were able to stay calm in a terrifying situation. I'm impressed."

In spite of everything, I can't help but feel flattered and feel my cheeks blush even though he can't see me. This is the most we have spoken to each other since I became empress. His voice still has the power to make me weak. It's a good thing I'm not trying to walk right now.

Riding the horse, though, is terribly uncomfortable. My thighs are already sore, as is my lower back. We are ambling along slowly, slower than a walking pace since the overloaded carts are being led by servants. I hold tightly to Honghui, afraid I might slip off one side or the other of the horse. It's hard to keep my balance.

"How bad is it?" I ask. Honghui is quiet for a long time before answering.

"Bad. The fighting along the coast was devastating. Some of the fishing villages are completely gone. We didn't have many ships, but the few we did have were destroyed, at least those positioned at Dagu. There are some far to the south, but it would take days for them to receive any messages to come to Peking, and even longer for them to get here. For the moment, it is better that they stay where they are. We can't afford any more losses."

The road climbs steadily uphill. I turn around to get another look and see that we are a fair distance from the Forbidden City. From here, it looks as it always did—large, red, and impenetrable. The only hint that something is wrong is the plumes of black smoke rising from the city and the endless trail of people leading back to the city. Honghui said the foreigners did not want to sack the city, but the fire and mass of people fleeing tell another story.

"What happened?" I ask. "How did it come to this?"

He is quiet, and then shakes his head. "You wouldn't understand."

"Try to explain it," I say. "I am the empress, am I not? I should know what's going on, even if there is nothing I can do about it."

He says nothing, only focuses on keeping people from getting between the last cart and our horse. I lay my head on his back and listen to his even breathing.

"This is a conflict that has been brewing since my grand-father was emperor," he finally says. I stay quiet so he doesn't stop. "China has a lot of things the foreigners want: silk, porcelain, tea. A country is like any business, it needs money to run smoothly. So, we allow the foreigners to trade with our people, as long as our people and the foreigners pay a tax, a fee, if you will, to the government."

So far, his explanation does not seem overly compli-cated. It must be a lot of goods, and a lot of tax, that is exchanged in order to keep us living in the opulence we do —we did. I wait for him to continue, to find out what impact this will have on us.

"But the foreigners are greedy," he says. "They want lower taxes, their own ports, their own cities where their people won't have to follow our laws. They want to bring in missionaries, religious people, to try and convert the people to their way of thinking and turn them against us.

"We have tried to come to agreements where we can. After all, we need to make money somehow. But every time we make a concession, they then push for more. They push and push, just to see how much they can take from us before we push back.

"When it was only the British, we were able to set limits on what we thought was reasonable. England is a very small country. But other countries have seen how rich England has grown through trade with us, and now they all want their share. What we give to one country, all the others want as well. They have been carving out pieces of our land for their own, where they set their own rules, including tax regulations, to get away with paying us less and less. We are losing our country and our income bit by bit."

He sighs. "The latest round of treaty agreements were far too unfair to us, so Guozhi pushed back. He refused to sign them and threatened to expel the foreigners altogether. The bluff worked, and the foreigners pulled back. They issued new treaty agreements more in line with what we had agreed to in the past. But Guozhi thought that the previous agreements were too greedy as well. He thought that this was an opportunity to take back some of what we have been forced to give in the past. He refused to sign the treaties, issuing new ones of his own that strongly curtailed the foreigners' rights. He thought he had the upper hand. That since the foreigners had backed down once, they would back down again. But he was wrong.

"Instead of backing down, the foreigners threatened to take what they wanted by force. They said that Guozhi was corrupt and greedy and didn't deserve to be emperor. That they would depose him and put someone else in charge."

I snort, but do my best not to laugh. Two hundred years ago, the Manchu invaders did much the same. The previous emperor had grown weak, and there was much unrest. So, the Manchu, barbarians from the far north, invaded and put their own Manchu emperor on the throne. The fact that the same thing is happening to the Manchu makes me laugh inside, though I wouldn't dare do so in front of Honghui. I'm supposed to be playing the part of a fellow Manchu. I am the Manchu empress. I should be horrified by what is happening. But, really, should the foreigners run all of the Manchu out of China, I wouldn't be sorry. It would be unfortunate that yet another foreign power would be on the throne, but it makes no difference to me. One conqueror is pretty much like the next.

"I suppose the foreigners made good on their threats," I say. "They have pushed Guozhi out and put their own emperor on the throne?"

"Not quite yet," Honghui says. "They wanted to show Guozhi that they could, indeed, do what they threatened. They could appoint their own emperor if they wanted. But they don't really want to go that far."

"Why not? Why would they walk away from a victory?"

"The one thing we have on our side is our size," he says. "China is a massive country. All the other countries could fit inside China and there would still be room left over. They don't speak our language, understand our ways. If they tried to appoint their own emperor, the people would fight back. There would be an uncontrollable rebellion."

I am skeptical at this. I don't know anyone who would fight and die for the Manchu emperor. But maybe I am wrong. Perhaps a Manchu ruler is at least preferable to someone from across the sea.

I look at those around us who have fled the city, afraid for their safety. They are tired, dirty, and growing weary. Many have stopped and are sitting on the side of the road. Bags and animals and other items have been abandoned along the way, too much for the people to carry.

"So, what now?" I ask.

"We will go to Jehol," Honghui says with a defeated sigh. "The emperor and his advisors will draw up new treaties and we will all work toward an agreement that will let us return home."

"What if an agreement still cannot be reached?" I ask.

"I do not think that will happen," he says. "We might not be happy with the terms, but Guozhi will have to come to an agreement sooner or later."

"But what if he doesn't?" I ask. I wait a long time for an answer, but one doesn't come. I'm not sure if this means it won't happen, or that he doesn't want to tell me if it does. I don't press him for an answer. There is nothing I can do about it either way. I won't be consulted in the negotiations. I don't even know what countries we are fighting against. I am glad to at least now understand the severity of the situation, but that is all. I can only go to Jehol and tend to my duties as empress of the harem as best I can and hope that Guozhi and the foreigners come to terms soon so that we may return home.

I hear a scream and crash from further up ahead and the line of donkey carts comes to a sudden halt. Honghui urges his horse ahead to find out what is wrong. We arrive to find that a wheel on one of the carts has broken, causing the cart to collapse to one side, throwing the ladies and their trunks onto the road. One of the trunks has burst open, sending silks and jewels and shoes and other items strewn across the ground. People passing by stop and steal whatever they can get their hands on. One of the ladies is screaming for help because her things are being stolen. Three eunuchs are fighting with the thieves, trying to get the items back while still more passersby take whatever they want. The other lady who had been in the cart is being tended to by her maids. It looks as if she hit her head in the fall.

I jump down from the horse and run to the injured woman. I hear a gunshot and see that Honghui has fired his gun into the air and is now pointing it at the thieves. He orders them to drop the items and move along. Some do as they are told, others just run, pilfered goods and all. Honghui then uses his horse and gun to keep the crowd from getting too close while I try to figure out what to do.

The injured lady has a small, bloody gash on her forehead, but I do not think it is deep. Her maid holds a handkerchief to it to stop the bleeding. The eunuchs then turn the cart upright and try to fix the wheel, but it is hopeless.

"We will just have to walk, then," I say.

The girl who lost everything whimpers in horror. "But it's so far!"

"If your servants are capable of walking the distance, then you are too," I tell her. "I will walk as well. Honghui, take this injured girl on your horse."

He nods as the eunuchs help him pull the girl up in front of him in the saddle so he can keep his arms around her and make sure she doesn't fall. The donkey is released from the useless cart, and the remaining trunk is strapped to its back. After the cart is cleared from the road, we are moving once again. The concubine whines and protests about having to walk, but I ignore her. The other carts follow along behind us and I watch as the carts that had been ahead of us pull farther away.

The people who have fled Peking along with us look at us from time to time, especially the concubine. I dressed plainly, and I am sure I am filthy and stink of horse. I probably look like all the other refugees. The concubine, however, is wearing a fine, embroidered, silk qipao and is still wearing her headdress. How she managed to not lose it when she fell from the donkey cart is beyond me. She did at least heed my order to wear flat shoes, but she lets us know every time she steps on a rock or twig. The passersby watch us with indifference, confusion, disdain, and humor. They say nothing to us, but I fear what might have become of us without Honghui's protection. We surely would have been robbed of everything, even the clothes we are wearing, at the very least.

The walk is long and arduous. My own feet and legs are sore, but I try to keep my discomfort to myself. We keep walking, not even stopping at night except to feed and water the donkeys. I have the ladies take turns riding on the remaining donkey carts and walking.

After what I think has been two days and two nights of walking—I may have lost count—I am surprised to see Jinhai coming toward us, leading empty donkey carts, enough for each lady to have her own cart. They must be the carts that arrived ahead of us. I nearly collapse into his arms and cry with relief. He holds me and pats my back.

"There, there, my lady," he says. "All is well." He helps me into a cart and my legs immediately go numb. If I couldn't see them, I would swear I had lost them on the journey.

With the carts lightened by having to carry only one

lady and at most a single trunk, we are able to make the final part of the journey at a quick pace.

Finally, a mountain rises before me, and at the top is a solid, gray wall, the outer wall of the Winter Palace. It is nothing like the Forbidden City, or the Summer Palace, places of green trees, blue waters, and bright colors. Even though this place is called the Winter Palace, it is a military fort. Plain, strong, and practical.

It is beautiful.

16

Once we get through the main gate of the outer wall, I can see that the Winter Palace is not as plain as I thought. Built on the side of a mountain, the palace rises ever higher, each building on a tier higher than the one before it. It is arranged so that you are always walking either uphill or downhill, which is going to make it very difficult for the ladies once they are able to wear their pot-bottom shoes again. Like the Summer Palace, I can see no division between and inner court and outer court. The entire palace is open, filled with paths, evergreen trees, and ponds. Right now, it is warm, and everything is in bloom. But come winter, the palace will be blanketed in thick snow, or so I have heard. But winter is months away. We will surely be back home—I mean, in the Forbidden City—by then.

The large main courtyard is full of ladies, all crying, talking, and embracing one another. The trunks are stacked and the poor donkeys are led away to be fed and watered in nearby stables. As I climb out of my own cart, so exhausted I want nothing more than to find a bed and sleep, the ladies throng around me.

"What are we to do?"

"Where should we go?"

"When can we eat?"

So many questions, and I have answers to none of them. I look around, but I do not see Honghui. Nor do I see the emperor. That single thought recalls the burning anger I feel for Guozhi that has been building within me over the long trek north. How could he be so foolish, so selfish, as to put us in this position? He led us to war, and then left us to fend for ourselves. And now that we have managed to find our way here, we still have no directions about what to do.

"Where is Fiyanggu?" I ask Jinhai. He asks around, and soon Fiyanggu is kneeling before me. I touch his shoulder to bring him to my height. I'll not talk down to him when I need him so. "What are we to do?"

He shakes his head. "I'm not sure, your majesty," he says. "In truth, I don't know that the harem has ever been brought here before. It is a hunting lodge. Past emperors would come here to get away from the pressures of palace life—including the ladies."

I have to restrain from rolling my eyes at this. The emperor has the entire outer court, half the Forbidden City, to himself where we ladies are not permitted to enter. There are many nights, sometimes weeks at a time, where he summons no ladies to his bed-chamber. The thought that the emperor needs an entire palace to himself hundreds of li away from the women he chose to marry irritates me beyond measure.

"The palace was not designed to house palace ladies, and certainly not so many. The emperor himself has not been here in many years, so there are very few supplies—"

"Now that you have outlined the problems," I say,

folding my hands together tightly, "what solutions do you suggest?"

His face blanches and his jaw drops as if he didn't expect me to ask such a thing. But who else can I ask? I have no idea what the palace has to offer, or where we can get supplies. Fiyanggu stammers, something about room assignments and locating the servants.

"The ladies are hungry," I say. "They have not eaten in two days, at least. First, find them something to eat. Then we will worry about where they will sleep tonight."

Fiyanggu bows and backs away. "Yes, your majesty."

I turn to Jinhai and ask for his suggestions.

"We need to find out who is here," he says. "We need to make sure all the ladies arrived safely, and their servants. Some of the ladies have already complained about missing servants. I am certain some fled in the chaos."

I nod. "Take an accounting here in the courtyard," I say. "Arrange the trunks so that the ladies have somewhere to sit, and make sure no one is sick or injured. Let me know about any problems you encounter."

"Yes, your majesty."

Jinhai and his assistants move through the crowd of ladies and servants, doing his best to organize them in some way.

"Majesty," Suyin says to me. "There is a room ready for you."

"What?"

"I have spoken to the servants who are always here at the Winter Palace. This place is seldom used, but it is maintained should the emperor wish to use it. It was not prepared to house the entire harem, but there are rooms for the emperor and the empress that are well-appointed."

This news comes as a relief, but knowing that there are

so many ladies around me who have nowhere to go leaves me hesitant to take advantage of it.

"The empress dowager is already settled in a palace of her own," Suyin adds. Of course, Fenfeng would make sure she is comfortable regardless of the troubles facing the rest of us. I try not to let it bother me, though. Better she is comfortable and out of my sight than uncomfortable and making trouble for me.

"Thank you," I say. "But there is too much to do to rest now. Make sure Yanmei and the girls are settled there for now."

"I have already done so, your majesty," Suyin says. "I knew you would want to make sure the children were tended to first."

The relief I feel that at least something has been done right is enough to nearly knock me over. I grip Suyin's arm and nod.

"Majesty," she says, leading me to a trunk to sit on. "Are you unwell? You should rest."

"No," I say. "I can't. The other ladies—"

"Your majesty." I look up to see one of Guozhi's eunuchs kneeling before me. "His majesty requests your presence."

I nod and Suyin helps me stand again. I follow the eunuch into one of the buildings toward the front of the palace. It is the largest building, so far as I can tell. The building is very plain. In the Forbidden City, every column, every beam, every bit of woodwork is engraved, painted, and lacquered. There are rugs everywhere, and heavy curtains hang over windows and doors. The Winter Palace has none of this. Its walls and floors are grey stone and there are no decorations of any kind. I stand outside a door as several of Guozhi's advisors leave, including Honghui. He seems to not see me, though, and his face is troubled.

Once they have passed, I am led into the room and the doors are closed behind me. This is Guozhi's bed-chamber. Unlike the rest of the palace, this room is decorated. A large, comfortable-looking, kang bed is in the middle of the room. There are two braziers, both burning brightly even though the room would be warm enough without them. There are rugs on the floor and curtains on the windows. It looks nearly identical to his bed-chamber back in the Forbidden City.

But what I find most irritating is that Guozhi does not look like a man who was just forced from his home, from his city. He is wearing a yellow, dragon robe and his queue is freshly washed, oiled, and plaited. I see several empty bowls of food and rice that have not been cleared away yet and my stomach growls. I grit my teeth to keep from speaking out of turn. He looks at me with an eyebrow raised. I am so angry, I forgot to bow. I drop down.

"Forgive me, your majesty," I say, doing my best to sound humble. "I forgot myself. I am exhausted from the long journey."

He motions with his hand that it is acceptable for me to stand once again. "I am glad you have arrived safely. According to reports, all the ladies have arrived and are unharmed. You did well, Lihua."

"Thank you," I manage. "They are in need of food and rest. The palace was not prepared for our arrival."

"I am sure everything will be sorted soon enough," he says dismissively. I chew my lower lip. It is as if he is trying to make me angry. "My mother is rather unhappy, though. She said that you did not let her bring any of her necessities. Is it true you set fire to her things? That was very poorly done."

"There were barely enough carts for the ladies," I say.

"The few we had could not be wasted on dresses and shoes."

"Lihua," he says in a warning tone. "She is your mother-in-law. You must respect her position and age. If a few fineries bring her comfort, you should have made allowance for them."

I can hardly believe what I am hearing. "You would prefer for me to have left some of the women behind so that your mother might have a few more gowns to wear?"

"I am sure that you could have found another way," he says, turning away from me and pacing the length of the room. "But I know I expected a lot from someone so young. You didn't know that you should be prepared for any possibility."

"You told me everything was fine!" I say, almost yelling. "You told me that the foreigners would never even reach Peking, much less the palace. You gave me no notice of what was happening. No indication that I should prepare to evacuate."

I don't tell him that I was at least prepared for myself and his children. He doesn't need to know that his brother took better care of his family than he did.

He shakes his head. "As soon as I knew that things had taken a turn for the worst, I sent for you and the others. You were all able to get out. I am glad of that. But you should be more level-headed in the future."

"We could have died!"

He scoffs. "You exaggerate."

"I saw them!" I say. "I saw the foreigners. They broke into the inner court. I saw their pale and hairy faces. Their blue uniforms. They carried guns. One of them grabbed me and..." I shudder at the memory. Up until now, I had been so intent on surviving, I have not had time to feel afraid. But

I can see his yellow teeth, smell his breath as he pulled me close to him.

I wipe my nose and wrap my arms around myself. "I have no doubt that if they had caught me, caught any of us, we would have come to a bad end."

He opens his mouth, I think to chastise me again, but he seems to think better of it. "I did not realize that you saw them. How did you escape?"

I shrug. Does he not know that Honghui saved me? It is no secret. Many people saw me riding on the back of his horse. Guozhi will surely find out. Will he be angry with me? Thankful to his brother? I have no idea.

"The...the foreigners did not pursue us," I say. "They seemed content with occupying the palace."

"At least they have some honor," he says. He is then quiet for a long time. I don't look at him, but keep my eyes downcast, squeezing my hands together.

"I am glad you—all of you—are safe," he finally says. I let out a long, low exhale, trying to let my anger out. I do not accept his words, but fighting with him will accomplish nothing.

"What will we do now?" I ask him.

"You should return the harem," he says. "The women need your guidance, I'm sure."

"No," I say. "I mean, what is the plan for ending this war quickly and getting us home?"

He waves his hand. "Don't worry. I will take care of that."

"That's what you said before," I say.

He turns and looks at me sharply. "What did you say?" he demands. He heard me clearly and is already angry. I want to yell and scream. Tell him how incompetent he has been. Tell him how much danger he put us all in. Tell him that we are hurt and frightened. That I don't trust him to get us back home. Ask if we need to prepare to flee again.

But I say none of that. After all, he won't be truthful with me. He will continue to tell me everything is fine no matter how close to collapse we are. His advisors, his brother, might know the truth, but for him to lose face, look weak, in front of his women is a blow he cannot face.

"I...I only want to know how long we should plan to stay here," I settle on.

"Indefinitely," he says. "Help the ladies get comfortable. They might have to stay here for some time."

"I will do as you say." I give a bow and back out of the room. I don't look to see if his face is angry or not as I leave. It doesn't matter right now. He has far more to worry about than an insolent woman. He might decide to punish me later, after we return home. It is more likely he will have forgotten all about me by then.

When I return to the courtyard, I am heartened to see that all the ladies are seated around a large pot of rice. There are also pots of simmering meats and vegetables. Not a lot, but it appears to be enough. The ladies all have bowls and chopsticks and are eating eagerly.

"How did this come about?" I ask as Jinhai comes to me with a bowl of my own. The rice alone makes my stomach growl, but the stewed meat, so tender, so flavorful, is enough to make me forget my manners as I shovel the food into my mouth.

"The palace has cooking staff on hand," Jinhai explains. "Not many. Usually just enough to care for the servants who are stationed here year-round. But they had some food on hand and started preparing it as soon as we started arriving."

"That was smart of them," I say.

He nods. "Many of the cooks from the Forbidden City have arrived as well. And they had the wherewithal to bring bags of staple foods. Rice, flour, beans. It is enough to get us by for now until we are able to figure out how to get more food sent up."

I stop eating long enough to take a breath and sigh. "Good. Take note of the cooks who brought supplies. Once we are settled, I will see them rewarded."

He bows and goes to...do whatever it is he is doing to help get us organized and settled. When all the ladies are fed and have a place to lay their heads, I know it will not be my doing, but that of the eunuchs. I will have to find ways to show my appreciation for all they have done for us.

I look around and notice that the mood in the courtyard has altered. The women no longer seem scared, and they certainly are no longer hungry. I see that most of them have their hair down and are wearing flat shoes. Their clothes are disheveled and dirty. There is a distinct smell of donkey in the air. Despite all that, they are sitting together, laughing and talking. It seems that, for the moment at least, shoes, and jewels, and gowns, and rank, and appearance have little meaning. We are all together, safe and alive. And that is enough for now.

"Your majesty!" Fiyanggu rushes toward me and kneels at my side. "There is a problem."

"What is it?"

"The Lady Huiyin, she is not here," he whispers in my ear.

My stomach sinks at this news. "Are you sure?"

He nods. "I've checked everywhere. No one has seen her. Her servants are not here either."

I rub my forehead and try to recall if I saw her among

those lined up for a donkey cart. Everything was so chaotic, I cannot remember seeing anyone in particular.

"What are we to do?" I ask. "Can we...can we send someone back for her?"

"I will have to speak to the emperor," he says. "It will be up to him what we should do. It would not be prudent for me to send people to the Forbidden City while the foreigners have it occupied without the emperor's protection."

I nod as tears fill my eyes. Huiyin was—is—such a kind woman. I will be devastated if something has happened to her. Why didn't she try to get a cart? Did she flee on her own? Was she hiding? Is she in the Forbidden City still? I feel sick as I think of what might become of her should the foreigners find her. Their wild eyes and bushy faces will haunt my dreams for years to come, I am sure.

The worst part is that I failed her. I was the one who left without making sure all the ladies were safe and accounted for. Whatever terrible things befall her will be because of me. I'll never be able to forgive myself.

17

———

_L_ife in the Winter Palace is miserable. It is so crowded, the ladies are crammed four and five to a palace, some even having to share beds. They fight over space. They fight over clothes. They fight over makeup. The servants fight. There is enough food to go around, but it is far less than everyone is used to, so people are hungry. The women quickly spend what money they were able to smuggle out of the palace on bribes and gifts in order to receive special treatment, but there is no special treatment to give, which leaves the ladies penniless and even more frustrated.

I share my palace with Yanmei, the girls, and my servants. My palace is, of course, larger than all the others, and I could house more ladies, but the girls need some protection from what is going on. Some semblance of normalcy.

The emperor does not keep me apprised of the situation, so I do not know if the negotiations are going well or not. Will we return home? Or will we have to flee again?

Will the Manchu be overthrown? Honghui said that the foreigners did not want to remove Guozhi from the throne, but I am sure that they did not want to invade Peking initially either. I could be wrong about that. If China has many things that the foreign people want, they might be planning to simply take the country by force no matter what the emperor does. I cannot begin to imagine what that would mean for the people of China.

The empress dowager is no help to me. In fact, she seems to relish how miserable I am. Every time I see her, there is a smug smile on her face I wish I could slap off. But, of course, I cannot. I must play the dutiful daughter-in-law. After Guozhi criticized me for choosing his consorts over Fenfeng's shoes, I do not trust him to stand by my side and support me in any conflicts with his mother, so I am doing my best to avoid her altogether. Fenfeng has a palace all to herself, which at least keeps her away from me most of the time. I know that some of the consorts who are unhappy with the answers they get from me are turning to Fenfeng, but there is nothing she can do either, so I'm not particularly worried.

After weeks at the Winter Palace, I am surprised when Guozhi summons me to his bed-chamber one evening. He has summoned none of the women to him since our arrival. I am hoping that this is a good sign. If he is feeling relaxed and confident enough to make love, perhaps the negotiations are going well.

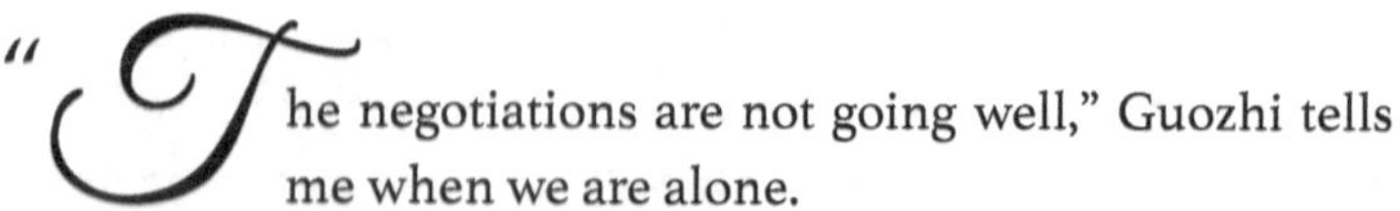

"The negotiations are not going well," Guozhi tells me when we are alone.

"Majesty?" I ask, confused. He is still fully dressed, so it seems that he did not bring me here to perform my wifely duties. Why am I here, then?

"The foreigners have refused to concede on a single point," he says, shaking his head. "I have ordered my general to prepare for open war."

This terrifies me. After what Honghui told me about the foreigners joining forces against us, I don't see how one nation, even one as strong as ours, can stand against the rest of the world.

"What does this mean?" I ask before I let my imagination run away with me.

"Don't worry," he says. "I am sure we will be victorious. But it will be a long and bloody ordeal."

"Bloody...?" I say, my own blood draining from my head. I feel woozy and slump onto a nearby chair. "The women... The consorts... Their brothers and fathers and cousins, the ones who have been recruited already... Are they going to die?"

"You must not let the other consorts know what is happening," he says firmly. "They will not understand."

"Then why are you telling me?" I ask. I thought I wanted to know what was happening, the truth of the situation. But now I think I should have been kept in the dark. There is nothing I can do to help, so why inform me?

"Because I must leave tomorrow—"

"Leave?" I yell, jumping up from my seat. He holds his hand up to silence me.

"I must leave tomorrow to lead the troops."

"No!" I say. "You cannot put your own life at risk like that."

"Lihua," he says in annoyance. "Please, just listen."

I sink back onto my chair.

"The consorts will surely hear of my leaving. They will suspect the worst. I need you to help them remain calm."

"Again?" I say. "Is that all I am good for? To lie to your women and keep them placated until we must flee again?"

"We will not flee again," he says. I open my mouth to argue, but then think better of it.

"You should not fight," I say instead. "You are too important to the empire. To us."

"I won't be fighting," he says. "I will ride ahead of the troops and meet the foreign generals face to face. They will surely come to a truce when they see how large our army is. When they see that I will not back down from defending my country."

I shake my head but say nothing. I put my hand to my mouth to make sure I say nothing. I know almost nothing of this war. It is surely more complicated than I can understand. But I still think this is a bad idea. It seems as though every decision Guozhi has made has only pushed us deeper into conflict. I do not see how this will turn out any better for us.

Perhaps Guozhi is in the right. Maybe the foreigners are being too greedy. Maybe they are pushing their ways on us and turning the people against the emperor. But I don't think that having a less prosperous country is worse than having no country at all. If Guozhi were to concede, at least we could go home. The other problems could be dealt with later, right?

But what does my opinion matter? I am just a stupid, poor girl from a Han family. I shouldn't even be here, much less worried about what happens to a foolish Manchu emperor. But even as I think it, guilt settles into my stomach. I don't want to be a Manchu empress, but neither do I want to see my friends and family killed or deposed. Guozhi has been good to me, and I think he is taking what he believes to be the best course of action. I love Yanmei and Suyin and Jinhai. They have become family to me. And what of Dongmei and Jingfei? I am the only mother they have left. I cannot let anything come between us. Then, there is Honghui. If I could marry him legally, I would.

For all of my life, I wanted the Manchu empire to fall. I was taught to hate everything about them. But I am now so torn. I still think the Manchu have no right to the throne, a throne they stole. But neither do I wish death and destruction on them. I love them, and I know they love me. I must do whatever I can to help the Manchu survive. At least for now.

I have forgotten what Guozhi and I were even talking about. I have had a hundred different thoughts since he last spoke. I clear my throat.

"Is that all?" I ask. "You want me to keep the women calm in your absence?"

"There is one more thing," he says. I wait for him to continue, but he hesitates. He pats the bed, inviting me to sit beside him. I go to him, but sit some distance away.

"I will come back to you, Lihua," he says. "I promise."

I nod slowly.

"But I am not a young man anymore. And anything could happen to me at any time. A horse could throw me and my life would be over."

"What are you—"

"A son, Lihua," he says. "I must have a son. There must be an heir to the throne should the unthinkable happen."

My mouth opens and closes on its own. "I...I'm sorry I am not with child—"

He holds up his hand to stop me. "I know that you are

not. And neither are any of the other ladies, according to Fiyanggu. But even since Caihong…" He shakes his head before the memory can carry him away. "Life has held very little joy for me. I have not had…had much motivation to fulfill that part of my responsibilities."

I place my hand on his. "Life has been very difficult, for all of us. I am sure you have done what you can. Lady Yanmei has spoken very highly of her time with you."

"Has she?" he asks, surprised, and I nod. "She is a sweet girl. I had hoped that she would fall pregnant, but maybe it is not meant to be. I have a hundred wives and only two worthless daughters to show for it. And the only one of my women to carry a son died because of it. Maybe I am not meant to have a son. My line is not supposed to continue. Maybe Heaven is punishing me for some slight against them."

"I'm sure that's not true," I say. "You've always been the best emperor you know how to be."

He scoffs. "Maybe that is the problem. I don't know how to be a better emperor. The emperor the country needs."

"That's not what I meant."

"I know. But there could still be some truth in it. I have often wondered if Father should have appointed Honghui as his heir instead of me."

"What?" I ask. "Why? You were the oldest."

"That doesn't matter," he says, looking at me as if I should know this. "It is the responsibility of the emperor to choose the most capable heir. At the time of his death, I thought that he made the right choice. But now, all these years later, after time to reflect, I think that he could have made the wrong choice."

"You have no cause to think that," I say.

"Don't I?" he asks. "Honghui is the smart one. The calm one. He is the one pushing for me to accept the treaties."

"You still could," I say. "Honghui doesn't need to be the emperor. He could be right where he is supposed to be —*advising* the emperor."

"It's too late for that," he says. "I cannot reverse course now."

I want to shake him, shout that of course he can change course. He's the emperor! He can do whatever he wants. But I know he will not listen to me.

He looks at my face and I think he sees the frustration there. The anger. The disappointment. He clears his throat.

"I have said too much," he says. "None of this is your concern. I only brought you here tonight for one purpose."

"Oh?" I ask, raising an eyebrow. I'm not sure I want to hear the answer.

"I must do my best to have a son, no matter the situation."

I gulp. The idea of having to be intimate now, at such a moment, after such words have been said, fills me with dread. His words make me wonder just how much he is keeping from me. Is he really worried about dying accidentally? Or is it something else? Does he think that he will not return from the battle that is surely coming? Just once, I wish he would tell me the truth.

I want to argue. Protest. Assure him that he will come back. Tell him that this is not the time. But as he said, he brought me here for this one purpose. In truth, he didn't have to tell me anything. My only duty as empress is to give the emperor a son. Caihong died fulfilling that duty. I can do this much.

I untie my robe. As I remove it, Guozhi softly touches my shoulder. First with his fingers, then with his lips. He gently lays me back on the bed. There is a kindness in his movements. The way he touches me, kisses me. But there is a sadness as well. The act is over quickly, and he does not send me away after. I fall asleep in his arms.

In my dreams, I hear the thunder of running horses, the clashing of swords, and the singing of bullets.

18

It is still dark when I am woken by the light of braziers and the shuffling of many feet. The emperor is standing in the middle of the room as his eunuchs dress him in his battle armor. I sit up and expect to be dismissed. Instead, while the eunuchs work, Guozhi speaks to me.

"How well do you know the history of our people, Lihua?" he asks.

"Not well, your majesty," I admit. He nods, his arms held outstretched to his sides as a eunuch helps him into what looks to be a thick, yellow, silk jacket. But between the layers of silk, I know there are thin, iron plates.

"Before my great-great-great-grandfather became the first Qing Emperor," Guozhi says, "we Manchu were a strong people. A warrior people. We conquered the frozen lands north of the Great Wall with nothing more than arrows and spears from the backs of our ponies. We built ships and sailed across the sea to subjugate Japan and Chosun."

I didn't realize that the Manchu had invaded other

countries as well. I thought it had just been us. I wonder if those people are as oppressed as our own.

"We were an unfettered people then. Riding across the great, grass plains, our domain farther than the sun could reach. We were not constrained to palaces or walls or the fate of nations. Each of us, the eight banners, lived wild and free."

A eunuch ties Guozhi's armor closed in the front while another ties more silk and iron plates to his legs. A long strip of armor is wrapped and tied around Guozhi's neck as if to strangle him. He grimaces as he turns his head right and left, attempting to get comfortable.

A eunuch then walks forward with a tall, copper helmet. He moves to place it on the emperor's head, but instead, the emperor takes it from him and walks toward me.

"Even our women rode beside us in battle," he says. He offers the helmet to me. It is heavier than I expect. The helmet is gold in color, shimmering in the firelight of the braziers. On each side and the back are riveted more silk and iron plates. The silk is embroidered with blue, five-toed dragons and encrusted with jewels. Attached to the top of the helm, sticking up several inches, is a long, black tassel.

The emperor bows to me—*to me!*—inclining his head so he faces the floor. I place the helmet on his head, and when he looks at me again, he seems transformed. He is no longer the sad, frightened man I went to bed with last night, but the emperor he is meant to be.

"Come," he tells me. I follow behind him as we leave the bed-chamber and walk through the palace to the southern gate. Everyone, maids, eunuchs, advisors, noblemen, go to their knees and kowtow as the emperor passes by.

Through the gate, a dozen men on horseback, all in armor, are waiting, including Honghui. A ring of palace guards is holding back hundreds, if not thousands, of people, those who had fled Peking beside us and in the days after. They are dirty, hungry. I hear babies cry and see the tops of white tents where people have been living. I feel very guilty for ever having considered the Winter Palace crowded.

"May the emperor live ten-thousand years!" someone says.

"May the emperor live ten-thousand years!" a dozen voices then ring out.

"May the emperor live ten-thousand years!" the entire mass of people seems to say at once, the sound deafening.

A eunuch brings over a stool and helps Guozhi climb up onto the back of his muscular, black horse. The animal whinnies at the extra weight, but stands strong.

"This is not the end," he tells me, "but the start of a new golden age."

I step forward and take his hand in both of mine. "Come back to me."

"I promise, Lihua."

Someone yells out a command and the guards part. The horses form two lines as they leave the palace and head back down the long and dusty road to Peking. The emperor's hand slips from mine. Even among the large host of horses, I can still see the tassel at the top of his helmet, waving in the wind.

"My name is Daiyu," I whisper. My heart aches that he is riding off to war without knowing who he is really leaving behind. I regret never telling him, "My name is Daiyu."

I walk back through the palace, dreading the chaos awaiting me. I'm in no mood to deal with petty bickering. To my surprise, though, the palace is completely silent. I don't know what the other women and palace servants have been told, if anything, but there is a heavy sadness in the air, dampening all noise. Not a bird tweets, not a cricket chirps. There are very few ladies out of their palaces. Those who have ventured out are alone, sitting, thinking. They look at me when I pass by, and I expect them to reach out to me, but they don't.

At the courtyard of my palace, I finally hear chatter. Jingfei. She is sitting with Yanmei by the pond, tossing bits of a steamed bun to the koi. Dongmei is there also, but she says nothing. I sit with them and pull Jingfei to my side.

"Look at the blue one, Mama," she says. "We don't have blue koi at home."

Her words catch me off guard and I freeze for a moment. It is the first time she has called me "Mama." I hadn't asked her to. She had a wonderful mother, and I want Jingfei to remember her. I look at Yanmei, who gives me a smile and reaches over to take my hand. I give it a squeeze, and then we go back to watching Jingfei and the fish.

"What do you think Wangli is doing right now?" Yanmei asks me, her voice barely above a whisper.

I hesitate, not sure that this is something we should speak of. I look around, and see that no one is standing very close.

"I don't know," I say. "The last letter must have held instructions of some kind. Telling her where to meet him or something. According to her parents, she never returned home. So Wangli and her lover could be anywhere."

"If they are caught, do you think anyone will tell us? Or will it be kept a secret since it is so shameful?"

"Someone will tell us, I think," I say. "The punishment will be used as a warning to us all."

"Can you imagine loving someone so much that you would face death for him?"

I shake my head. "No." I took a great risk the few times I was with Honghui after I became a consort to the emperor. But I thought it was a very small risk. I was no longer a virgin. And if I fell pregnant, the emperor would believe the child was his. After I was elevated and the risk became too great, Honghui and I did not meet again. I miss him, but I would not die for him.

"I'm not pregnant," Yanmei says sadly, wiping a tear from her cheek. "I know everyone hoped I would be since I spent so much time in his bed lately. But it has been too long since I was with him."

"I'm sorry. But there will be more opportunities. He will call you to his bed again."

"Will he?" she asks, her eyes glassy. "Do you truly believe he will come back?"

"I have to. I cannot imagine life otherwise. What would happen to us?"

Yanmei's eyes widen and I know she is imagining the worst. All of us taken and given to the foreign invaders as war prizes. The lucky ones murdered; the unlucky ones... I shudder to imagine it.

"He promised me," I say. "He promised to come back."

Yanmei is quiet for a long moment. "Then he is certain to return. Heaven will make sure of it."

We are quiet again for some time. I don't know how long. I am terrified of the future. My life has been in a constant state of danger from the first time I met Mingxia. I feared being discovered and put to death every day. But that was nothing compared to the uncertainty I feel right now.

Before, my life could only follow one of two possible paths. I would either remain hidden and live a long, comfortable life, or I would be discovered and most likely put to death. There was a bizarre comfort in the knowing, even if one of the paths ended up with my head removed from my body.

I try to shake the thoughts way. Working my way through every possible eventuality is an endless and exhausting process. I stand up and clap my hands.

"Come, girls," I say. "We cannot stay here, wallowing in sadness. Life must continue. Have you done your lessons for the day?"

"No," Dongmei answers.

"Have you done them at all since we left Peking?"

Dongmei doesn't answer, which means no.

"Very well. Where are your books and ink and brushes?"

Dongmei shrugs. I then realize that all of their supplies were left behind. I packed clothes for them, but I didn't think about the little things. Paper and ink. Their favorite toys. I have no idea where their tutors are.

I call Jinhai to me. "Find paper and ink. This palace must be stocked with some supplies."

"Indeed, your majesty," he says. "The emperor's office will have such items." He gives a bow and rushes off.

"What is the point?" Dongmei asks with an irritated sigh. "Who will teach us? We don't have any books."

She makes a good point. I cannot read or write, so I cannot teach her. But then an idea comes to me.

"You will teach me," I say. Dongmei stares at me, as if she is waiting for me to tell her that I am joking. When I don't, her tough exterior cracks and a smile crosses her face.

"Really?"

"Yes, really," I say. "You are much smarter than I am. I could learn a lot from you."

Dongmei's smile gets wider, perhaps wider than I have ever seen it.

Jinhai returns with paper, ink sticks, brushes, ink stones,

and a bowl of water. We go to a sitting room and sit around a circular table. Once we are situated, Dongmei dabs her ink stick in the bowl of water and then rubs it around on an inkstone.

"You make the ink like this," she says.

"I have at least learned to make ink," I say, but I still follow her lead.

"I like the red ink," Jingfei says. Yanmei finds a red ink stick and hands it to her.

"Don't get any on your clothes," Yanmei says.

Just the act of making ink, gliding the ink stick around the inkstone, trying to find the perfect consistency, is soothing.

"You should start by being able to write your name," Dongmei says, dipping a horse-hair brush into the ink. I have learned that much. Well, at least Lihua's name. Jinhai and my other tutors have been doing a good job teaching me. But I don't tell Dongmei this. She seems to be enjoying herself, and I don't want to take that away from her.

Dongmei uses her left hand to hold her sleeve back as she begins writing with her right hand. She holds the brush straight, upright, and writes each stroke perfectly. "Li-hua" is made up of two characters. There are eighteen strokes in the first character, and eleven in the second one. I might know how to write my name, but Dongmei does it so much more quickly, the strokes seem to appear by magic. And her writing is far more beautiful than my own. I am almost embarrassed to show my seven-year-old teacher my work. She laughs when she sees it.

"I don't think you wrote your name," she says.

"What?" I ask, looking at my work. I guess I did miss a stroke, and some of the strokes run into each other. "I must have gotten too much ink on my brush. What did I write?"

She wrinkles her nose as she studies the characters. "It looks like you were trying to write 'pretty flower.'"

"Oh. Well, at least it is something nice and not smelly pig or something."

This time, both of the girls burst into laughter.

"Lihua's name means smelly pig!" Jingfei says, laughing so hard she nearly falls off her seat.

For the rest of the afternoon, the girls and I write and draw and make fun of my terrible writing. By the time I put them in their beds to go to sleep, they are exhausted and drop off quickly. Oddly enough, I sleep well, too. A deep, restful sleep that gives me the strength to face the days ahead.

19

———

I am helping the girls with their lessons when a commotion so loud I can hear it in my palace breaks out. There is screaming and yelling, horses whinnying, and gunshots. My worst fears come to the fore, that the emperor has lost the war and the foreigners have come for me.

"Yanmei, take the girls to my room and lock the door. Let no one in or out until I return."

"What is happening?" Dongmei asks. Jingfei begins to cry.

I kneel down and hug both of the girls to me. "I am going to find out. Try not to be afraid. I'll return soon." Yanmei takes the girls by their hands and leads them away.

"Your Majesty," Jinhai says, "you should hide yourself away as well."

"No," I say. "With the emperor gone, there is no one else to give instructions. I need to know what is going on so I know what to do next."

He bows and follows me out of the palace. I walk down a path toward the noise. It is coming from beyond the east wall. Several palace ladies are also outside, trying to see what is happening.

"Back to your palaces," I tell them. "Lock the doors until I say otherwise."

Many of the ladies hesitate and have to be led away by their servants. I understand the strain of not knowing what is happening around them, but I don't want them to get in the way, get lost, or be left behind should we have to flee again.

As I near the wall, the noises become clearer. The shouts are of men and women, and I hear children crying. There is no army outside the walls, only the people of Peking who fled the danger.

"What is going on?" I ask Jinhai. "Why are the people screaming?"

He shakes his head, but another eunuch comes running over. He kneels before me.

"Majesty, the people have started to revolt."

"Why?" I ask.

"They fled with only what they could carry," he says. "They have run out of food. Very few have any shelter. They blame the emperor for their troubles." I hear another gunshot.

"Who is shooting? Are the people going to storm the walls?"

"No, Your Majesty," he says. "The palace guards have had to shoot some people who broke through the line in an attempt to get the emperor's attention."

"What? The guards are killing our own people? Make them stop!"

"But-but-but, your majesty, they will surely beat down the gate if we don't stop them."

"They are hungry and cold," I say. "Their children are starving. They need help, not to be shot at."

The eunuch stammers, looking to Jinhai for help, but he only shrugs his shoulders.

"What would you have us do, your majesty?" the eunuch asks.

"Go to the kitchens and collect whatever food you can find," I say. "Give it to the people."

"What?" he asks, his face blanching. "You would have us starve?"

"We will not starve if we do not eat for one day," I say. "We have been getting regular food deliveries, have we not?"

"Yes, your majesty. We were able to source food from local farmers to provide for us."

"There you have it, then," I say. "Give what we have to the people. We will worry about the rest later."

"Yes, your majesty," he says before running off.

"Jinhai," I say, "tell the guards to stop shooting. Make an announcement to the people that relief is coming."

"I will see what I can do," he says. I watch him leave and then pace, wringing my hands as I wait for the commotion to die down. Instead, though, the commotion seems to grow louder. At least the gunshots stop.

I see Jinhai coming back toward me. "What is happening?" I ask him.

"The people do not believe relief is coming," he says. "They have been begging for help for days."

"Days?" I exclaim. "Why was I not told?"

"Well...umm...this is not something that would normally be brought to your attention."

I sigh and pinch the bridge of my nose. This is the first time that the emperor, the prince, and all of the emperor's advisors have been out of the palace at the same time. Since there is no man to report to, I suppose the eunuchs have just been sitting on the information. I try not to blame them since this is so unprecedented, but I am still annoyed.

"Where is the food? They will believe you if they see it."

"It is being gathered now," he says. "But it will not go far. I fear that those closest to the gate will take the majority of it."

I close my eyes and pace. I fear he might be right. As soon as the people see bags of food, they will rush the servants and take whatever they can. Hunger can make the most generous man a selfish beast.

"Fine," I say. "Divide the food into small batches. Tie small amounts up in bags and that is what we will hand out."

"It will take time," he says.

"Then get busy," I tell him. "Bring a basket of parcels to me as soon as you can." He bows and rushes away. I return to my own palace and call Suyin to me.

"I told you not to bring my phoenix crown with us," I tell her. "Did you obey that order?"

Her face blushes and she looks down. "I...I'm sorry—"

"Do you have it?" I press, not wanting apologies. "Is it here?"

"Yes, my lady. I just couldn't leave it behind. I hid it in the bottom of the case with your robes."

"Bless you," I say, relieved.

"Majesty?"

"Help me dress, quickly."

She bows and we go to my room. Yanmei must unlock the door for me.

"What is happening?" she asks.

"It is the people, the refugees from the city. They are starving and begging for aid."

"That's terrible," she says. "What are you going to do about it?"

"Feed them," I say, "from our own stores."

"But-but-but, what are we to eat?" she asks.

"I will worry about that later," I say as Suyin wraps a yellow robe around me and ties it closed. I sit on a stool as she affixes the phoenix crown to the top of my head.

"What are you doing?" Yanmei asks.

"I am taking the food to them myself."

"No!" Yanmei and Suyin both say at the same time.

"It's too dangerous," Suyin says.

"Doing nothing is too dangerous," I say. "The people think that the emperor doesn't care about them. That he will let them starve. If we do nothing, they will surely pull the walls down around us. Give me some of the bags of cash we brought."

Suyin goes to my kang bed and pulls a small bag out. Then she goes to a trunk and pulls out another one.

"They will rob and kill you!" Yanmei says, and Dongmei and Jingfei start to cry.

"No, they won't," I say. I remember being so poor that we had almost no food to eat. I remember being resentful of the Manchu for keeping so much food for themselves. How they had so much money, they could live in a palace while we shivered together in huts. I remember what I told Prince Honghui when I collected my own money as a consort to give to the poor. Even a small amount of relief can make all the difference when a person has nothing.

"I will return soon," I tell Yanmei. Suyin helps me walk in pot-bottom shoes for the first time in what feels like weeks. I could go out in a maid's outfit, or even that of a concubine. I could choose to not go out at all. But I want the people to know that I do care about them. That the Manchu care. That the emperor cares. What good will it do to defeat the foreigners only to have a revolt here at home? I hope that by seeing me, their empress, the people will know that they have been heard and that I will help them.

As I make my way back to the main gate, the empress dowager tries to stop me.

"What do you think you are doing?" she demands.

"Exactly what you probably have already heard or you would not be here," I say. "I am taking relief to the poor people outside our walls."

"No!" she says. "This is completely undignified. An empress should never mingle among the common folk. It is disgusting. I forbid it."

I laugh. "You know you cannot stop me."

"I will tell my son about this as soon as he returns," she says. "He will not be pleased. He will be horrified."

"Then he can tell me that himself when he returns."

Two eunuchs come toward me with a large basket. Inside are small burlap bundles tied with what looks like pond reeds. They must not have had enough string to tie them and made do.

"You are debasing the crown," Fenfeng goes on. "Demeaning the emperor! You must stop this."

"Each bundle has a handful of rice, then we put vegetables or a bit of meat in each one," one of the eunuchs tells me, all of us ignoring Fenfeng's protests. "It's not much…"

"It will be better than what they have now," I say. "Come."

"You will regret this, Lihua!" Fenfeng calls after me. "You will no longer be empress when the emperor hears of it."

"I hope that is a promise," I say, turning my back to her

and walking to the gate. If the emperor strips me of my position and title for giving food to the poor, I will know I did the right thing.

The large gate is opened for me and I step outside. The guards are still holding the people back, but they are struggling. Still, some people are able to see through them at me.

"It's the empress!" someone says.

"Manchu pig!" another person yells.

"May the empress live ten-thousand years!"

"Down with the Manchu!"

Some people drop down and kowtow, others shake their fits at me. For a moment, I do wonder if I have made a mistake in coming outside myself. I have put myself in great danger. I cannot stop now, though. I take one of the parcels from the basket and put it into one of the hands grasping between the guards. The person stands back, confused. He squeezes the bag.

"Rice?" he asks.

"And more," I tell him.

"Food!" he yells. "The empress has food!"

The people then begin screaming and pushing forward even harder, crushing toward the guards in front of me. Dozens of dirty hands reach for me, clawing.

"We should retreat, your majesty!" Jinhai says, tugging on my shoulder. But I shrug him away and take no heed. I reach into the basket, pulling out parcels one after another, putting them into as many hands as possible.

"Help me!" I tell Jinhai. He hesitates, but then he pulls a parcel out of the basket and hands it to the nearest person to him.

"Thank you, your majesty," someone says.

"Bless you, my lady," another says.

"May the empress live ten-thousand years!" I hear

several voices cry out. Slowly, the crowd puts less pressure on the guards. Soon, though, the basket is empty and there are many groans of disappointment.

"More is coming," I tell them. "Please be patient." I reach into my sleeve and pull out a gold coin. I press it into one of the still grasping hands. I hear a startled gasp.

"Her Majesty is truly generous!"

I know it isn't food, but I am hoping the people can use it with the nearby farmers and in local towns to buy what they need. I give out a few more coins before Fiyanggu comes out of the gate, followed by eunuchs with two baskets of wrapped food.

"Help me," I tell him. He and the other eunuchs pick up bags and hand them to the waiting people. The process is slow, and out of the hundreds, if not thousands of people who have gathered, we cannot reach very many of them. I tug on the shirt of one of the guards. "Move."

He steps aside hesitatingly and I move into the crowd, handing out parcels and coins to all those I can reach. As people take things from me, they hold my hand as long as possible. Some people cry. Some people give thanks. Some people kiss my hands. Some people say nothing as they turn away with their prize. I smile at each one of them as I work, expecting nothing in return except for the rioting to stop.

Finally, I reach into the basket for another parcel but find it empty. I look up at Jinhai, who shakes his head and holds his hands out helplessly.

"That's all there is," Fiyanggu confirms.

I gulp. I hadn't considered what I would do when the food ran out, which it was sure to do eventually.

"I'm sorry," I say to the people around me. "There's none left."

A groan of disappointment washes through the crowd. Some people cry. Some stomp away in anger. Some yell obscenities and shake their fists at me. But, to my surprise, the vast majority of people drop to their knees and kowtow to me.

"May the empress live ten-thousand years!" they repeat, almost like a chant.

The fear I felt a moment ago melts away and I am filled with a sense of calm. My own eyes fill with tears, but I cannot stop smiling.

"We love you, empress!"

"May Heaven bless you!"

I have spent the last year wondering why I was here. Why I had been selected. Why Heaven would allow a Han woman to be chosen as empress. Maybe this is the reason why. Who better to understand the needs of the people than someone who is one of them? Perhaps none of this has happened by chance, but was my destiny.

"We should go back inside," Jinhai whispers to me, tugging on my arm. "Leave while you have their goodwill."

I nod and let him lead me out of the crowd back toward the palace. "I will try to bring more food tomorrow," I tell them. "Please know that I am doing my best to help you while my husband, the emperor, may he live ten-thousand years, defends us from the foreign threat."

The crowd cheers and sings my praise as I retreat into the palace and the great gates are shut behind me. I slump down onto the first bench I see, my energy suddenly fleeing.

"Do you think it will make a difference?" I ask Jinhai. "Will the people stop revolting, at least for now?"

He looks back toward the gate and we listen as the crowd continues to cheer.

"I think it made all the difference, my lady."

"There is still much to do," I say. "We must find more food. I need to tell the ladies what is happening." I try to stand, but he places a hand on my shoulder to stop me.

"Rest, your majesty," he says. "Fiyanggu and I will sort everything out. You have done enough."

I shake my head. "Not nearly enough." But I don't try to stand. I'm not sure I could if I wanted to, my legs feel so weak. Jinhai gives me a smile and nod and backs away.

I take a few breaths and hear the cheering start to die down. But shouts of anger do not take their place. I can only hope that they are dispersing for the night, making use of what I was able to give them. I have no idea if we will actually have more food to give them tomorrow or not. It is impossible to know what each day will bring. But I was able to help the people now, and buy us another day. I must be content with that for the moment.

20

Every day, several servants go out into the local villages, markets, and countryside and scout for food. Whatever they bring back, we divide it into half, saving one half for those of us in the Winter Palace, and dividing the rest into small parcels for the people outside. The Winter Palace is currently home to hundreds of people when accounting for all the servants. They need food just as much as the people outside, so I cannot allow them to go hungry. Still, the food is hardly enough, and I fear that the crowd outside the Winter Palace, which seems to grow every day, will not be satisfied with the little I am able to give. There have been no more riots, but there is a tension in the air that seems to grow day by day. I do not know how long it will be before the people finally snap.

Even though it is hard work, and the dowager still forbids me from doing it, and I am sure the emperor will be displeased when he finds out, I enjoy my time with the people each day. The people who come to me for food are less harried than they were that first day, so I am able to at least share a smile or kind word with each person I meet.

They thank me, hold my hands, and kowtow before me. I try to be gracious, but the praise makes me uncomfortable.

I wish so much that I could tell them who I am. Not a Manchu lady made empress, but one of them. A Han Chinese. A poor person from the hutongs. A person who knows their struggles. But I cannot tell them. At least being with them—with people who are like the real me—gives me a sense of peace. I feel as if, just for a little while, I can let my guard down.

I am outside with the people when we hear the thunder of horse hooves. The guards clear the road as I see the emperor's men returning.

"Hurry, inside, your majesty!" Jinhai tells me. I drop what I am doing and rush inside with him ahead of the cavalcade. There will be no way to hide from the emperor what I have been doing, but I can at least not be caught outside the palace walls. All of us kneel in the courtyard and wait for the emperor to appear. Most of the ladies come out of their palaces and kneel as well.

The men rush inside and pass us without even acknowledging me. Honghui comes through, barking orders. I am about to stand up and ask him what is going on when I see two men carrying a stretcher. My heart seizes in my chest when I see that they are carrying Guozhi, who is clearly severely injured. His face is pale and his eyes are closed, his arm hanging limply to one side. The women all jump to their feet and start screaming and crying. Honghui, angered by the commotion, finally faces us.

"Go back to your palaces, all of you!" he yells.

The women quickly disperse, many leaning on the arms of their maids and eunuchs. More than one of them fainted. But I will deal with all that later. I go to Honghui and his expression softens.

"What has happened?" I ask, clutching the front of my robe, afraid to hear the answer.

"We are at all-out war," he tells me. "There is no hope for a treaty now."

All the air rushes out of me, and I lean on Jinhai for support. "Guozhi, the emperor, is he...?" I cannot even ask the words.

"No...not yet," he says.

"Not...yet?" I repeat. Honghui wraps an arm around my shoulders and leads me into the emperor's palace.

"Not yet," he confirms. "But he is badly injured. I fear..." He shakes his head. He cannot speak his true fear out loud, and I have no wish to hear it.

Guozhi has already been laid out on his kang bed as the eunuchs fuss around him, removing his clothes, washing him, helping to make him comfortable. I push forward through the crowd and kneel by the bed, taking Guozhi's hand in mine. It is cold. I see that his abdomen is wrapped in what was once white, cloth strips that are now nearly completely red. I fear that he is already dead.

"Husband," I say. "Your Majesty, can you hear me?"

Slowly, and with great effort, his eyes flutter open. He turns his head toward me. He opens his mouth to speak, but only a croaking sound comes out.

"He needs water!" I yell.

Guozhi lifts his hand, just touching my cheek with his fingertips, and then he loses consciousness.

"Your majesty!" I cry out, shaking his arm. "Your majesty!"

"Lihua..." I feel Honghui's hands on my shoulders as he tugs me away. There is the stomping of feet and I see several soldiers enter the room with the doctor, the same doctor who cut Empress Caihong open to deliver her stillborn son.

The soldiers must have brought him from Peking with them.

"Clear out, clear out!" the doctor says. "Let me work. He needs air. Everyone out." He points to two eunuchs to stay and help him, sending them for water and clean bandages. Most of the soldiers leave, except for one who appears to be of high rank. He probably wants to make sure that the doctor does his best to save the emperor.

Honghui pulls on me again, leading me from the room. Once we are in the courtyard, I sink onto a stone bench. Honghui sits on a stool near me.

The courtyard fills with people again and I see the empress dowager bustle past, surrounded by her entourage of servants and ladies. I stand up to stop them, but Honghui holds me back and shakes his head. I stay where I am while he goes inside. I suppose he will know better how to deal with his mother at this time.

I hear a scream and a cry. A moment later, the dowager, looking pale and frail, is practically being carried out of Guizhou's room by several strong eunuchs. She holds a handkerchief to her face, which looks several years older than it did the day before. I feel a surprising pang of pity for the woman. Cruel and cold as she is, it must be terrible for her to see her child laid out like that.

I stand and then kneel as Fenfeng is carried past me, doing my best to appear respectful. This is not a time for us to fight. I have no idea if she even saw me since she says nothing to me as she and her people all leave the courtyard.

I stand and see Honghui come out of Guozhi's room and walk toward me.

"What happened at the battle?" I ask.

"Guozhi would not concede," he says. "Not a bit. He thought he had the advantage. But when battle broke out

—" He shakes his head. "We were severely outmatched. Their guns are far more powerful than any we have. And every one of their men is armed. Our people, only a few have guns. Most expected a swordfight. And our armor—" His face twists from sorrow to anger. "I had no idea, but most of the men, their armor is merely woven rattan!"

"What?" I ask, thinking that this cannot be true.

"I am not the general, nor the head of the war council. I do what I am told in times like this, the same as any soldier. But I have good armor, real armor, so I thought everyone else did too. That seems to not be the case. Armor is expensive, and we have had no wars in two hundred years. For most of the people, the armor—" He shudders. "The armor was mainly for show. When the foreigners opened fire..." He gets a haunted look on his face as he looks out into the courtyard. "It was a slaughter, Lihua. Our men fell long before they reached the enemy."

"The emperor," I say. "Was his armor woven?"

"No," he says. "But it is old. It's the same armor our ancestor wore when he first rode into Peking to take the palace from the Ming."

I shake my head. I cannot believe that Guozhi would risk his life, risk his country, for the sake of honoring an ancestor that stole China hundreds of years ago. Such foolish pride!

"What is happening now?" I ask. "There is a war, but the emperor is here, injured. What are we going to do?"

"If we are lucky, the foreigners will be here in a matter of days," he says.

"If we are lucky?" I ask, horrified. "How can that be lucky?"

"If we are unlucky, the foreign armies will take their time," he says. "They will mow down our troops and then pillage the countryside. They might send troops to other major cities to take them. Thousands will die, if not millions."

I have to turn away and hold my hand to my mouth. I am near to vomiting. How could this happen? How could Guozhi allow this to happen?

"What will happen when the foreign army reaches us?"

"They will take the fort," he says. "They will then force Guozhi to sign a treaty at gunpoint. It will not be much of a treaty, though. It will be an abdication of power."

"And if he refuses to sign?" I ask, as this seems the most likely outcome given Guozhi's actions so far.

"They will kill him and force me to sign it."

"And will you?"

He doesn't answer. I'm not sure if it is because he doesn't want to tell me the truth or if it is because he doesn't know himself yet.

"Is there a way to stop this?" I ask. "Any way to still broker a peace? Even if the treaty is unfair, it will save millions of lives."

"There is a treaty on the table," he says. "Guozhi can sign it at any time. If he were to do that, then I could take it to the foreign leaders and this would all be at an end."

"But he will never do that," I say. "Not now that he has come so far."

"Exactly."

I give him a long look, begging him to hear me ask the question that is treason to speak aloud. I think he hears me, but he will not tell me what I want to hear if I do not ask him.

"And if the emperor dies?" I finally say.

"I would sign it," he says with almost no hesitation.

I look away, my eyes watering. I don't want to wish for

the emperor's death. I don't want Guozhi to die. I don't want my country to be forced into an unfair treaty. My people are oppressed enough by the Manchu. I can't imagine how difficult their lives will be if even the Manchu are oppressed.

"There has to be another way," I say. "There has to be!"

"I wish there was," he says. "But I cannot disobey my brother, my emperor."

"Your stupid pride!" I yell, jumping to my feet. "Your worthless honor! What good is it to us if we are all dead?"

"And what would you have me do?" he growls, standing up and facing me. He is considerably taller than me. I must crane my neck to look up at him. But I do not cower. I do not back down. Honghui doesn't intimidate me. I know him far too well.

"Sign the treaty," I say. "Tell them your brother is too injured to rule or make decisions. Rule in his place and save us."

He takes a step back and turns away from me. He runs his hand over his face. I think he might actually be considering it. I allow myself to hope, just for a moment.

"I cannot," he says, finally looking back at me. "Guozhi would never forgive me. He would probably execute me for treason."

"He's your brother—"

"All the more reason! I should be the person he can trust most in this world."

I don't know what to say to this. He's right, of course. As much as Guozhi might love his brother, I have no doubt he would see him put to death for such an egregious injury. Guozhi's pride will always reign over his love.

"Besides," Honghui goes on, "he would just invalidate the treaty at the first opportunity and we would end up in the same place again."

I cannot refute this. I sit back down on the stone bench. There is nothing we can do to stop the foreigners from coming. From overtaking the Winter Palace. What will happen to us? To me?

"What can we do now?" I ask. "What should we be doing?"

"We need to seal the gates. Put as many men between us and the coming armies as possible."

"We cannot knowingly send men to be slaughtered."

"We need to buy time. We must shore up as many supplies as possible. Food and barrels of water. There will be a siege. We have to continue putting up a fight for as long as possible. Maybe a solution will present itself that I cannot see yet."

"What about the people?" I ask. "There are thousands of people outside the wall who came here thinking that the emperor would protect them. Will we bring them within the walls?"

"Certainly not!" Honghui says. "We will be short on supplies as it is."

"So...they will just be left to fend for themselves? Left to be pillaged and murdered?"

"We can't save them, Lihua," Honghui says. "We can't stop what is coming. Only Guozhi has the power to do that, and he will not do it."

I am at once disgusted and terrified. All those people, women, children. People I have been giving food and money to just to help them weather a storm I thought would come to an end. People I gave hope to. How can I let them die now? But what can I do?

"Your majesty, your highness," a eunuch says, bowing to us both. "The emperor is awake. He wishes to speak to the both of you."

21

I allow Prince Honghui to enter the chamber ahead of me. The room is quite dark, but a brazier is burning, making the room stiflingly hot. I have to tug on the collar of my robe for a bit of air, but it doesn't help much. There are dozens of joss sticks burning, filling the room with smoke and the scent of musk. As strong as the smell is, though, it is unable to mask the rusty scent of blood, a scent I haven't smelled this strongly since Empress Caihong died in my arms. A monk kneels on the floor, bowing repeatedly, uttering a chant with his voice too low for me to understand him.

As I approach the emperor's bed, I suddenly stop and can move no closer. It is as if some invincible force is preventing me from taking another step. Honghui, however, moves closer without stopping. From where I am standing, I cannot tell if Guozhi is breathing, and I fear he is already dead. Is it wrong of me to feel a small sense of relief? If he were dead, Honghui would be emperor and this war would be at an end.

A weak cough from the bed tells me that Guozhi still

clings to life. He starts to utter something to Honghui, but his voice is small and I cannot hear what he is saying. I force my feet to move and I stand at the foot of the bed.

"...hold them back as long as possible," Guozhi is saying. "The road is narrow. We can pick them off as they come through the pass."

Or they can pick us off instead, I think to myself. *It is our people who would be slaughtered with such a tactic!*

"I will do my best, your majesty," Honghui says. "But I will not be able to hold them off forever. You know this—"

"Do not question me!" Guozhi strains to yell at his brother, but he devolves into a fit of coughing, then he grips his abdomen in pain. I go to a table and pour him a cup of water. I stand beside the bed, opposite Honghui, and help the emperor drink.

"Do not strain yourself, your majesty," I say. "You should reserve your strength."

"Do not worry, Lihua," he says. "I will recover. I'll not let the foreigners have the satisfaction of having done me in." I help him drink a little more, then he lays back on his pillow with a sigh. "I do not suppose you know if you are carrying my heir?" he asks after a long moment.

I shake my head. "I do not know. It is still possible. I anxiously await any signs."

He starts to nod, but even that much movement seems to pain him.

"Your majesty," Hinghui says, "I would not be doing my duty if I did not try one last time to persuade you to sign the treaty."

Guozhi scoffs. "You know my position on that."

"But if the foreigners have to take the Winter Palace by force, countless lives will be lost."

"Including the people outside," I add. "The refugees from the city who came here for protection."

"They should have stayed in their homes," Guozhi says. "They should have defended the city to the very last man. Instead, they fled like cowards."

I grit my teeth and turn away from him, putting the cup back on the table hard. There are able-bodied men in the crowd, yes. But they are trying to protect their families. There are far more women, children, and elderly persons outside than strong, young men. Does he expect children to carry swords against an army?

"Your majesty. Brother," Honghui tries. "I do not want to see you lose your country."

"Nor will I become some puppet of imperialist dogs!" Guozhi says with more fore than I thought him capable of. "Those people are nothing more than foreign barbarians!"

"So are you!" I whirl around and yell. My heart is racing and my fists are clenched. I thought I had said the words to myself, but as Guozhi and Honghui look at me, I realize I said them out loud.

"I mean, so am I. So are we." I am fumbling for the right words. "All of us. The Manchu. Hundreds of years ago, your —our—ancestors were nothing more than barbarians behind the wall. They invaded China and took what was not theirs."

"How dare you?" Guozhi hisses at me, coughing, gripping his stomach.

"Lihua—" Honghui says with a warning in his voice. But I'll not stop now. This entire affair is foolish and a waste of human lives and I'll not let it happen without saying my piece.

"What if all this is a punishment for the two-hundred

years of suffering for the Han people?" I say. "What if this is divine judgment from Heaven?"

"What do you know of it, foolish girl?" Guozhi says.

"Far more than you think," I say. "I'm—" I try to tell him the truth. Tell him that I am Daiyu. That I am a true Chinese, unlike him.

"Be silent!" Guozhi orders, stopping me. "Get out of my sight. You have dishonored me. You bring shame to your own people. You are the empress of China, yet you speak like a traitor. Be gone! I'll listen to your serpent tongue no longer."

Guozhi turns away from me in his bed. I try to speak again, but Honghui grabs my arms and pulls me away, out of the room, closing the door behind us.

"Are you mad?" Honghui asks me when we are outside again. "He could order your death for that! He will certainly demote you."

I bark a laugh. "You said yourself, either he will die from his injuries or the foreigners will kill him after they have taken the fort. What can he possibly do to me?"

"Far more than you give him credit for," Honghui says, worry on his face. "He still commands the army, the guards. He could order your death right now. Why don't you think before you speak, Lihua?"

"And how can you stay silent?" I ask. "How can you let a man who is delirious with pain and power bring about the fall of us all? Manchu and Han will die when the foreigners arrive. How can you stand here and do nothing?"

"Because that is my position!" he says. "I am the brother to the emperor, not the emperor himself. Heaven did not favor me, it chose him. I must follow him—to the very end if necessary."

My eyes water and fear settles into my stomach like a stone. "Then you are a coward," I say, my voice cracking.

Honghui's eyes glisten and he runs his hand over his chin, taking a step back from me. "Don't do this, Lihua. Don't say that."

"Why not?"

"Because I love you," he says. "I need you by my side for whatever happens next."

I suddenly feel very guilty for calling him a coward. It was unkind, and not true. I know he is not a coward. He is one of the bravest men I know. A man who has saved my life more than once.

Honghui pulls me into his arms and I lay against his chest as I cry. I feel his body shake and know he is crying too. He kisses the top of my head and holds me tightly.

"What will become of us?" I ask.

"I don't know," he says. "But we will face it together." He turns my face to his and kisses me. His kiss is sad and hungry and mirrors my own.

"Let's run away," I say when I pull away from him, my breath panting, my arms around his neck.

"What?"

"Get a horse and some supplies and let's run away. Leave this place. If Guozhi will let China fall, we don't need to be here to see it. Let's run far away from here. Somewhere the foreigners can't find us. We can take the girls, too. We could be a...a family."

He looks down at me, his fingers tense on my back. He opens his mouth, but then thinks better of it and looks away.

"I can't, Lihua," he finally says in a near whisper. "I can't leave him."

I should not have expected otherwise. I nod and lay my head against his chest again.

"You could," he says.

I look up at him. "What?"

"You could leave," he says. "It would be safer for you. Guozhi wouldn't be able to punish you that way, and the foreigners wouldn't be able to find you either."

"No," I say. "I can't leave you here alone. Besides, I can't leave the others, my servants, my friends. The children! I couldn't leave them behind, not ever."

He hugs me tightly and kisses my forehead. "Oh, Lihua. If only I knew what to do. Some way to avoid the coming battle."

"You'll think of something," I say. "I'm sure of it."

A voice clears, and we look up to see Fiyanggu standing at the entrance to the courtyard, his eyes downcast. Honghui and I practically push one another away.

"The emperor is...not doing well," I say. "I was crying. His highness was just trying to comfort me."

"Of course," Fiyanggu says, but I cannot read his expression. Does he believe me? Does he not believe me but will look the other way? Will he use this against me later?

"The ladies are anxious for news since the emperor's return," Fiyanggu says. "What should I tell them?"

"I'll speak to them," I say. "Please, give me a moment." Fiyanggu bows and backs away out of sight.

"What will you tell them?" Honghui asks.

"I don't know," I say. "Some lie, I suppose. Words of comfort that will lose all meaning as the army draws closer."

"If anything changes, I'll tell you immediately," he says. I nod and turn away. I look back just before I exit the courtyard and am sure the pain in his face is reflected in his own.

What am I to do? I wonder as I walk back to my palace. What *can* I do? If Honghui has no idea how to stop this war, how could I ever have a chance at coming up with a plan?

A eunuch leading a donkey cart crosses my path. As the animal brays, something prickles in the back of my mind. It is as if I have forgotten something, something important. Something I need to remember. But what?

I enter the courtyard of my palace and see one of the trunks that I had packed back at the Forbidden City in preparation to flee. The prickling gets stronger. But what is it? I can't flee again. Not now. Where would I go? What would happen to me and the girls? And what about Honghui? He needs me.

I slump down onto the trunk and look out over the courtyard. The grass is trampled. The fishpond is half empty of water. A stone bench is cracked and a stone stool is overturned. I hadn't noticed how much this palace had fallen into disrepair. It had seemed so beautiful before. A sign of hope. Honghui had said that we would be safe here, safe from the war, safe from the foreigners. He said that if I were captured—

I jump to my feet as I remember what he said. That was why I had planned to flee in the first place. Honghui had said that if I were captured, Guozhi would have to sign the treaty because he would not be able to withstand the shame of having his empress held hostage by his enemies.

I know what I have to do.

I run to my room and find a bag. I take my phoenix crown from my dressing table and place it gently inside. I then shed my fancy robe and put on the plain garments of a maid. I need to wear something more practical. Something I can ride a horse in.

Suyin enters the room as I am tying a belt about my waist. "Your majesty, what are you doing?"

"Shh!" I say, running to her. "I'm leaving."

"What?" she shrieks. I slap my hand over her mouth and shake my head. "What?" she asks more quietly.

"It is the only way to stop the war. To stop the foreigners from destroying the Winter Palace. It is the only way to get the emperor to sign the treaty."

"What are you talking about?" Suyin asks, and I realize she doesn't know any of what Honghui has told me about the situation.

"I can't explain it all right now," I say. "I just need you to trust me."

"But, you are leaving," Suyin says. "Leaving us? Leaving the girls?"

"I can't take you with me, but I will be back, I promise."

"Where are you going?"

I want to tell her my plan, but should she be interrogated, I don't want to get her in trouble. "The less you know, the better," I say. I sling the bag with my crown over my back. "But I am going to stop this war myself."

"What? How?"

"I can't tell you," I say. "You'll find out soon enough."

"My lady..." Suyin follows me back to the courtyard, her eyes wet with tears. "Let me go with you!"

"No. I don't want to put you in danger."

"But if it is dangerous, why are you going?"

"Because I am the only one who can," I say. I turn back to her and squeeze her arm. I then give her a hug. "Thank you for everything you've ever done for me."

Suyin holds me tightly, as though she would force me to stay, but I remove her arms from around me and back out of the courtyard. I know she is watching me as I run away, but

I don't look back. If I stop for even a moment, I might lose my courage.

The guards open the front gate for me immediately. They probably assume I am going to visit the people and hand out helpful items like I have been doing every day for the last week. But that is not my purpose this time.

Once I am outside, I look around for a horse and see Honghui's magnificent beast tied up to a post. It is still saddled and reined. I walk over and put my foot in the stirrup and try to haul myself up. It's much more difficult to do on my own than I expected and nearly fall backward onto my rear end.

"Your majesty?" A guard has approached me curiously. "What are you doing?"

"There is something I need to do," I say. "An urgent assignment from the emperor."

The guard's eyes go wide. "Of course, your majesty."

"Help me onto this horse."

"Are you sure?" he asks. "Do you know how to ride? You could injure yourself."

"I'm sure I will," I say. "But I don't have a choice. Now, help me."

He nods and practically picks me up himself, tossing me onto the saddle. I lean too far to my right and nearly fall off. I catch myself, but nearly fall off the horse the other way instead. It takes a bit of wiggling back and forth to find my balance. This was much easier when I had Honghui to grip onto.

The guard unlashes the horse from the post and hands me the reins. "Hold tightly," he says. "Go slow so you don't fall off. Lightly tug the reins in the direction you want to go and the horse will obey."

"Thank you," I say. "One day, I will reward you for your

assistance." He steps back as I turn the horse around toward the road. I only hope I am able to make good on my words to the guard.

The horse walks slowly to the road, and I find it challenging to stay in the saddle. Hopefully I will be able to go faster eventually, but for the moment, I need to concentrate on staying upright.

"May her majesty live ten-thousand years!" someone calls out. I look up and see people smiling, waving, and bowing at me.

"Heaven bless you, my lady!"

"We love you, your majesty!"

My heart swells with the warmth coming from the crowd, and it gives me strength. I wave to the people as I nudge the horse to move a little faster. For several minutes, the cheering from the crowd grows louder, even though I am moving further away from them, before it finally starts to become more distant.

I realize that Honghui, and maybe even the emperor, will hear that I have left very soon. Honghui will probably send someone to take me back, if he doesn't come after me himself. I urge the horse a little faster, and then a little faster.

Soon, I'm gliding down the open road toward Peking. Toward the Forbidden City. Toward the invading barbarians. There is no going back.

22

It takes me two days to reach the city, only stopping to water the horse when I happen upon a creek. Each one of my bones feels taken apart and put back together again. I had no idea how difficult and painful it was to ride a horse at more than a walking pace for such a long period of time. I don't know how soldiers do it.

The city is not in as much chaos as I expected, but neither is the city in its normal state. Smoke rises into the air from smoldering ashes, ashes that used to be homes. The roadways are crowded with people, but no one seems to be going anywhere. They seem lost, unsure of what to do.

There are foreign soldiers everywhere, and they are all carrying guns. Groups of them are at every corner, and they are stationed every few feet along the roads. The people are giving them a wide berth, but they watch the soldiers warily, whispering to one another as their eyes bounce from soldier to soldier. I do my best not to stare at them, but it is difficult since I have never seen people like them before, other than that brief moment when they broke into the inner court. Their skin ranges in color from pale peach to ruddy, as if the skin is burnt.

Most of them, but not all, have facial hair, and their straw- and brown-colored hair sticks out from under their folded, black hats. They wear red and white uniforms that are turning brown from the dust. They don't appear to be wearing any armor.

As I approach the Forbidden City, the soldiers grow thicker. I'm still quite a distance away from the palace when they form a long, tight line, preventing anyone from getting any closer. As I approach, one raises his hand and grips my horse's reins. He says something to me in a language I don't understand and I realize a significant flaw in my plan: I don't speak their language.

I shake my head to tell him I don't understand. He repeats his words more slowly, but that doesn't help and I shake my head again. He scoffs and tugs on the horse's reins, turning him away from the palace. He then waves his hand to shoo me away. I turn the horse back around and point to the large red wall.

The soldier waves his hands. "No, no, no," he says. I can at least grasp his meaning. I can understand why they don't want to let anyone inside, but I need to find a way to tell them who I am. Someone here must understand my language. Otherwise, how were they negotiating with Guozhi? I don't want to show my crown to just any random soldier. They probably won't understand me, and they might steal it. Even the most ignorant person would be able to see it is of high value.

I put my hand on my chest and then point to the Forbidden City, trying to tell the soldier that I live there. If he can understand that much, maybe he will make more of an effort to communicate to try and find out who I am. He turns to the man next to him and they speak for a moment. The other one shrugs his shoulders and shakes his head. I assume he either doesn't understand or doesn't know what to do. The first man looks at me and again shoos me away. When I try to nudge the horse forward, he raises his gun at me. My heart seizes for a moment.

I hadn't considered that I could be putting my life in danger. I don't know why, but I thought that proving who I was would be a simple affair, and then I would be treated respectfully while Guozhi signed the treaty for my release. The chance that I might be shot on the street before even reaching the palace never occurred to me.

I wheel my horse around and trot away from the line of soldiers while I try to think about what to do. I lead the horse around the palace and see that there is not a single break in the line of men. I sigh as I realize what I have to do. I have to get inside. I only hope I don't get killed in the endeavor. At the east gate, I lead the horse a little ways from the soldiers. Then, I turn the horse about, kick him in the sides, and order him to charge forward.

The men ahead of me have very little time to react. I can see their eyes go wide when they realize the warhorse is running straight for them. Some of the men shout and wave their arms, as if a simple warning will be enough to stop me, but I let out a yell of my own, urging the horse to keep going. Several men move out of the way, but the one right ahead of me pulls the gun off his shoulder, taking aim straight ahead. I bend forward, hiding myself behind the horse's head and neck.

There is a crack, a yell, screams. The horse stumbles forward and I am thrown forward into the air. For a moment, it feels like I am flying. But then I am falling. I crash into the rough, brown earth so hard, the wind goes out of me and my vision goes black. I roll across the ground more times than I can count before coming to a stop on my stomach.

If I thought I was in pain before, it is nothing compared to the pain I am in now. I am unable to move, my whole body feeling crushed. But there is a strong, sharp pain shooting through my left arm. I cry out and dare to open my eyes. I can't see my arm, but I do see my horse. Honghui's horse. The poor creature is lying on the ground, a large, red wound right in the center of his chest oozing blood onto the ground. His eyes are open, but it is clear he is already dead. I hope he didn't suffer.

I'm soon surrounded by soldiers, each holding a cocked rifle aimed at me. Two men grab my arms and drag me to standing. I scream in pain. It feels as if my left arm is being ripped from my body. I look down and am horrified to see white bone protruding from the skin. I try to scream again, but I vomit instead, the men directly in front of me jumping out of the way.

One of the men shouts something and points toward the gate. I am carried inside, my feet dragging behind me. I'm nauseous and disoriented, so I am unsure which building they take me to, but I am soon lying on a flat table. I look up at the red and gold ceiling and the beams seem to be spinning, making me dizzy and more nauseous.

A soldier comes to my side and he opens a bag, a look of worry on his face. He says something to me, but I can't understand him and try to shake my head, but I groan as it feels like my brain is going to explode. He holds a finger in front of my face and moves it right to left. I follow it, but it makes me more woozy and I lean to the right to vomit again. The man doesn't seem bothered and pulls out a handkerchief, dabbing my mouth. It is then that I realize the man must be a doctor. He continues speaking to me in a calm, soothing voice. I don't understand the words, but the sound helps put me at ease. He reaches over and touches my left arm. I wince and tears fall from my eyes. He shakes his head and moves around me.

When he is no longer in my line of sight, I see two men across the room holding my bag. I'd completely forgotten about it. I try to raise my right arm toward it. The men notice and walk toward me.

"Mine. Mine," I say, even though I am sure they don't understand me. But to my surprise, they repeat my words. I nod. "Mine. Mine."

They pull the phoenix crown out of the bag. I can see that it has been bent and broken, and some of the jewels and enameled pieces have broken off. However, it is not destroyed to the point that they don't understand its significance, their eyes going wide as they look at me with wonder on their faces.

I feel the doctor poking and prodding me. I must have wounds in other places because I feel him pour a fiery liquid on different parts of my body. I cry out, but I don't take my eyes off my crown or the men holding it.

"Mine. Mine," I repeat like a mantra. The men speak to each other for a few moments. One shakes his head. The other then speaks more forcefully. They seem to be arguing.

"Empress!" I cry out. "I am the empress!"

The men go quiet. One rubs his jaw while the other gapes. I'm not sure if it because they are surprised that I am able to yell at them or because they understand me. One of them repeats the word "empress" in my own language.

"Yes, yes," I say, nodding. "Empress."

The men then speak to one another, and I hear them say "empress" a couple more times. Then one of them says "emperor" in my language, followed by "empress."

"Yes!" I say again. "Emperor. Empress. I am the empress!"

Finally, I see understanding cross their faces. They must at least have learned the Chinese word for emperor, so they are able to make the connection between the words "emperor" and "empress."

The men then speak to each other emphatically, not angry, but excited. Two more men join them, and they all talk and argue together. Finally, one of the men leaves, and I can only hope he is going to find someone with authority, and maybe even someone who understands both our languages and can tell them who I am. I allow myself to relax just a bit, but that seems to amplify the pain in my body.

I look back up to the ceiling. The spinning has lessened a bit, but the pain seems to be growing more by the second. Tears escape my eyes and run into my ears. I was so stupid. It's incredible that I'm not dead. I should be dead. Either from being shot before I even reached the line of soldiers, from falling off the horse, or from being shot after I hit the ground. These men, this doctor, have no reason to help me. They could have tossed me back into the street and left me to die. I could still die. I don't know how bad my injuries are, and they could be life-threatening.

The doctor appears at my right side again, going through his bag. I reach out and touch his wrist.

"Thank you," I manage to say through my tears. I don't know if he understands my words, but I am sure he understands the sentiment. He smiles and nods. He places one of his warm hands on top of mine. He says something soothing, even though I don't understand the words. He then clears his throat and speaks more seriously. I think he is trying to tell me what is happening, but, of course, I don't understand. Still, I appreciate the attempt.

The doctor moves to my head, turning it to face the right. He then moves to my left side and I feel him moving my arm. I think he doesn't want me to see what is happening, and my heart begins to race. I start to panic and can hardly breathe. The pain is intense, but my fear is stronger. Is he going to cut my arm off?

There is a sudden movement. A sickening *crack*! The pain seems to shoot from my arm to my heart. I scream and everything goes black.

23

———

It is difficult to open my eyes. When I do, there is not much to see. The room is dim, lit only by a single brazier. I try to lift my left arm to rub my forehead and wince as pain grips me. I look down and see that my arm is lying across my stomach, completely wrapped in white gauze. It feels like a piece of metal is tied to the underside of it. There is a sling around my neck, holding my arm steady.

I then remember the white bone sticking through my skin and shudder. I delicately slide the fingers of my right hand along my left arm. It doesn't feel like anything is sticking out anymore. The doctor must have fixed it somehow.

I try to sit up, but my head starts to spin, so I lie back down on my side. My mouth is parched and my throat is scratchy. I hear a noise and see a foreign man stand up from a chair on the other side of the room. I hadn't noticed him before. He is holding a gun as he walks toward me. I shrink back away from him. He says something in his own language before leaving through a door.

I push myself up, but it takes a great effort. Sitting up makes me sick, but I close my eyes and breathe through it, not allowing myself to throw up. The effort exhausts me all over again, so I lean against the wall and wait for the will to move to return.

I hear the door open again and someone walks into the room. When I open my eyes, I gasp, seeing someone I never expected.

"Huiyin?"

Huiyin, the older concubine who had befriended me after I became empress, is standing in front of me, looking far more regal than before. She is standing straight, her hands folded in front of her, her head held high. I realize that she is wearing one of my robes, one of my headdresses, and I am guessing one of my exceptionally tall pairs of pot-bottom shoes. I am so shocked that I don't even notice the foreigner standing beside her until he clears his throat.

The man is quite tall as well, taller than Huiyin despite her shoes. He wears a red and white uniform similar to the others that I have seen, but it seems to be of better quality. He also wears a red sash and his left chest is covered with many small medals. The biggest difference, though, is that his hair is totally white under his folded, black hat. I could not guess his age, but with hair like that, I think he must be very old.

"I suppose you thought I was dead," Huiyin finally says.

I shake my head. "I didn't know what had happened to you. Why didn't you escape with the rest of us?"

"I didn't realize you had gone!" she says, her voice rising. "You left me! I hid, like you told us to, but no one came to tell me that we were to leave."

I shake my head. "I'm sorry," I say, but my voice is cracked and horse. I rub my throat and try to clear it. The man says something to Huiyin and she brings me a cup of water from a table across the room.

"Thank you," I say after I drink the whole cup without taking a breath. Huiyin says nothing, but I can see that she is still cross with me. "I'm sorry," I try again. "I told the eunuchs to gather everyone together. I waited as long as I could. I thought you were among us. I'm sorry."

"It is no matter," Huiyin says. "General Pake has been very good to me." Her voice even and her words curt. I feel terrible that she was left behind, and I hope I can make her believe me, but I have to focus on the reason I came here first.

I look at the man next to her. So, this is the general. Most likely, he is the man I have come to see. I give the man a nod of acknowledgment. The man then says something to Huiyin and she nods.

"How do you speak their language?" I ask Huiyin.

"I've been here for weeks," she says. "I had to find some way to communicate. It's not difficult if you put your mind to it. Besides, one of their men speaks Chinese, and he helped me."

I nod. So that is how the foreigners communicated with Guozhi in the past. Huiyin says something to the general, and they converse back and forth for a moment.

"He knows that you are Empress Lihua," Huiyin says. "The men realized you were someone special when they found the phoenix crown in your bag. Of course, he had wondered if you were merely a thief, but I confirmed to him that I recognized you."

"Thank you," I say.

"He wants to know why you are here."

"Because I want this war to end peacefully," I say. Huiyin translates, and General Pake asks something else.

"Have you brought a new treaty with you from the emperor?" Huiyin asks on behalf of the general.

"No," I say.

"Then how do you propose to end the war?"

"I want the general to take me hostage," I say. "To use me as a bargaining chip to force Emperor Guozhi to sign the treaty."

"Are you insane?" Huiyin gasps, showing emotion for the first time. "You know that Guozhi will kill you for this."

I shrug, then regret it. Every movement is pain. "Perhaps. But if this war continues, it is the people who will pay the price. I cannot allow that to happen."

After some back and forth with the general, Huiyin says, "The emperor knew I was here. At one point, my return was offered as part of the agreement. The emperor refused. He said I was a worthless woman. Why do you think his attitude will change? You are just another pearl on a string."

Huiyin is panting, her eyes wild. There is hurt on her face, and I think she may cry. I don't want to hurt her further, but neither can I lie.

"That was very poorly done by the emperor," I tell her. "He never told me that. If I had known that you were here, being held prisoner by the foreigners, I would have tried to find a way to bring you back."

Huiyin sighs and shakes her head. "There was nothing you could do. Guozhi doesn't care about me. He doesn't care about any of us."

"I disagree," I say. "He has a hundred concubines...but he only has *one* empress."

Huiyin's mouth gapes and her cheeks go red as if I had slapped her. General Pake says something, and it takes a moment for Huiyin to collect herself enough to translate my words to him.

General Pake looks at me, rubbing his chin. He paces the room a bit. I assume he is weighing the truth of my words. Perhaps I am wrong and have allowed myself to be captured by the enemy for nothing. But he has to at least try, I should think. The general calls someone into the room, and they converse back and forth for a minute. When they are done, the general faces me.

"It is unlikely that this will change anything," General Pake says to me through Huiyin. "Emperor Guozhi is a stubborn man."

"I am aware," I say, doing my best not to smile.

General Pake gives a knowing smirk. "But we will see if we can somehow use your arrival here to our advantage," he says. "It can't hurt, at least."

"Thank you," I say.

General Pake hesitates, but then he says, "You realize that should Guozhi accept the treaty in exchange for your return, we will not be able to guarantee your safety. Once you return to him, you will be at his mercy."

I nod. "I know."

"In that case, you are a very brave girl, your majesty." He then bows to me. I am so surprised, I don't know what to do, so I just sit there like an idiot.

General Pake exchanges words with Huiyin, and then he leaves us alone. Huiyin stands silently for a moment, but I assume she wishes to say something to me or she would have gone with the general. I give her a smile and pat the bed next to me. After a moment, she sits at the very end of the bed, on the edge, as if she expects to have to jump up in an instant.

"I am very sorry you were left behind," I say. "When I heard you were missing, I was so distraught, but I didn't know what to do. I couldn't come back."

She lets out a sigh and her rigid shoulders soften a bit. "I know. And besides, as the general said, he did try to return me to his majesty, but he didn't want me."

"I am sorry," I say, reaching out and taking her hand. "I wasn't told that. I was only told that the emperor was refusing to sign the treaty. If I had known you had been taken captive, I would have insisted he find a way to save you. If the emperor does accept the treaty and take me back, I will take you with me."

"No," she says. "No, you can't. I can never go back."

"Why?" I ask.

"Because I'm General Pake's woman now."

I gasp. "What? I'm so sorry! Has he hurt you?"

"No!" she says. "Of course not. The general is a perfect gentleman. When his men found me and took me to him, he kept me safe. I was still untouched when he offered me back to the emperor. But after the emperor abandoned me, I was so distraught. I thought my life was over. But the general..." She sighs. "He was there for me. He was so kind. He let me have anything in the palace I wanted."

"Ah," I say. "I noticed that you are wearing my things."

She preens, touching her hair. "They do look better on me."

I shake my head and then laugh. When she realizes that I hold no malice toward her, she laughs as well.

"Eventually, the general asked me to join him in his bed, and I accepted. I am his concubine now."

"Really?"

"Yes. He has a wife back in England. Children. But he says that it is common for men in his country to have a concubine. But usually only one or two, not dozens. He says he will take me home to England with him. He is going to give me a palace of my own. He said that the concubines in

England don't live with the wives, and they raise their own children. Isn't that wonderful?"

I nod. "I am glad that he is good to you, and that you are happy."

She beams. "I am. Probably for the first time in my life." She touches her stomach. "I believe I am already with child."

I gasp and touch her stomach. "How wonderful! Congratulations."

"The general is very excited. He wants this war to come to an end quickly so that we may return to his homeland. He wants the child born there."

I consider this for a moment. "So, if I hadn't come, did he have a plan to end the war? Have I sacrificed myself for nothing?"

She shrugs. "I don't know the details. I don't know how he planned to win. But I do know that their weapons are vastly superior to ours. Our people would not be able to stand against the foreign army for long."

I nod and realize that Honghui was probably right about the foreigners marching to Jehol and taking the empire by force.

"I cannot believe you risked your life by coming here," Huiyin says to me. "You know that Guozhi will consider this to be treason. He will kill you when he has you back in his grasp."

"I've risked my life more times than you realize," I say. I wish I could tell her more. Then, I realize that I can. Maybe. She's no longer a member of the harem. She will be leaving the country soon. I open my mouth, but at the same time, the door opens and a man walks in carrying a tray of food. I'm instantly starving and my mouth waters.

"Eat," Huiyin says, standing. "Rest. I will let you know what happens."

"Thank you," I say. She nods and leaves the room. I'm disappointed that I am too much of a coward to tell her the truth. But I will be here for several more days, I am sure. Perhaps the opportunity will present itself again.

24

———

"You still look terrible," Huiyin says to me.

We are sitting at my dressing table in my palace within the Forbidden City. General Pake said that since I was the empress, I should be treated as such, even if I was technically their prisoner. I was moved to my palace and given plenty of food and drink. However, many of my personal items—clothes, shoes, headdresses, paintings, furniture, silk bed linens—were all gone. It seems that the foreigners ransacked the palace, taking anything they thought could be of value. Huiyin, though, had a large store of items—some of which were mine—which she gave to me to use. She seemed a little sheepish about it, but I didn't say anything. I didn't need such finery in the first place.

I look in the mirror and sigh. "I still feel terrible as well."

When I was thrown from the horse, the left side of my body took most of the brunt. My arm was broken, my face is bruised, and my left hip is so sore, it is still difficult for me to walk several days later. I lay my right hand on my left arm where the bone had punctured through the flesh. The doctor came to check on me yesterday, and he said every-thing will heal perfectly in time. But he also said that there will be a terrible scar. I am afraid of what it is going to look like when the bandages are removed.

Huiyin turns my chin away from the mirror to face her. She gives me a reassuring smile as she paints my face, putting extra over the blue and purple bruises to hide them. She tries to apply red paint to my lips, but she stops and huffs.

"You are trembling. Stop it."

"I can't help it," I say. I let out a long exhale to try and calm my shaking nerves. "The emperor is going to be so angry with me."

Huiyin nods. She is trying to make me look presentable because after only a couple of days of talks, the emperor agreed to sign the treaty as long as I was returned to him unharmed. However, the emperor is still unwell. So he is sending Honghui to sign the treaty with his authority and to collect me. I am to be returned to the emperor at the Winter Palace. After that, I am not sure what will happen.

Guozhi will be angry, that much is certain. Had I been kidnapped or captured by the foreigners, I could not be blamed for what has happened. But I wasn't smart enough to consider that. I left in the middle of the day, with guards and a crowd of people watching. He will know that I allowed myself to be captured intentionally—and he will certainly view it as treason.

But how severe the punishment will be, I can only imag-ine. He could demote me from empress and make me a concubine again. He could strip my rank entirely and send me back to my "mother" in shame. Of course if that happened, I could then return home...wherever home may be. I have no idea where my parents are or how to find them, but I would not stop looking for them until I found them.

The worst thing that could happen, though, is that he could order my death. He could order me to hang myself, like he did with Lady An. Or, he could have me executed. It is this last possibility that frightens me the most, and the one I think most likely to happen.

I gasp out a sob and drop my head into my right hand. What have I done? How could I be so stupid? So impulsive? And why? For what? I try to remind myself that it was to save the lives of the people, but why? I don't know them. They don't know me. They don't even know my real name. Would any of them sacrifice themselves for me? Of course not. They think I'm Manchu. I'm just as much an enemy to them as General Pake and the rest of the foreigners.

Huiyin pulls me to her and hugs me tight. "Shh, your majesty," she coos. "It will be all right."

"It won't!" I say, pulling back and wiping my face, smudging my makeup. "He's going to kill me. I know it!"

"You don't know that," she says, squeezing my hand tight. "He loves you, doesn't he?"

"He loves his pride more," I say. "He would even kill his own brother if the slight was egregious enough."

Huiyin shakes her head. "I don't think that is true. He will be angry, yes, but he is the emperor. He is wise. He will do the right thing."

"If he were truly wise we would not be in this situation," I say bitterly. "It never should have come to this."

Huiyin's eyes go large, as though surprised I would speak against the emperor so bluntly. She looks down at her hands and then dampens a cloth to wash my face so she can start the process of painting on my makeup all over again.

"Huiyin," I say, reaching out and taking her hand, "can I trust you?"

"Of course," she says. I shake my head.

"No, I mean it," I say. "I don't want you to say that just because I am your empress. I mean, can I truly trust you as a friend? As one woman to another?"

Huiyin puts the cloth aside and takes my hand in both of hers. She looks directly into my eyes as she speaks.

"It is my true desire that you will be the last one of my countrymen that I will ever speak to," she says. "As soon as the treaty is signed and Pake finishes some other business here, we will take the first ship that sails from Dagu Port heading for England. And I'll not look back."

I see only sincerity in her eyes, or maybe that is what I want to see. I'm so desperate to tell someone the truth, I might trust her even if she were to say to me that she will go straight to the emperor with whatever I have to tell her. But I believe her. Her life, her destiny, is waiting for her on the other side of the world.

"I'm not Lihua," I say, but it comes out as barely a whisper.

"What?" she asks, looking confused.

"I'm not Ula-Nara Lihua," I say more clearly. I'm shaking, but I go on. "My name is Daiyu, Hong Daiyu. I'm Han Chinese."

Huiyin drops my hand and leans back as if she has been burned. "What?" she gasps.

I nod. "Lihua's mother paid me to take her daughter's place at the selection. Lihua was her only child, and she was a widow. She didn't want to lose her daughter to the emperor. So she paid my father a lot of money for me to stand in as Lihua because we looked similar."

Huiyin shakes her head as if she can't believe what she is hearing, her mouth gaping but no sound coming out.

"I was told that the chance of me being chosen was very small," I say. "I'm not nearly as refined or cultured as real Manchu girls. I thought I would fail at the very start. I didn't want to be chosen, never imagined I would! I didn't mean for things to go so far."

Huiyin is speechless. She turns away from me, turns back to speak, and then looks away again. I stay quiet, waiting for her response. Waiting for her to change her mind and walk away. Send word to the emperor of my deception.

"But...you're the empress," Huiyin says. "How...how is this possible?"

"I didn't want that to happen," I say. "It was all an accident. I didn't know that making Prince Honghui a stupid gift would elevate me. I didn't know that saving Caihong's life would elevate me again. I didn't know that she would... that she would die. I tried to hide among the ladies, disappear. I never wanted to go to the emperor's bed. I wanted him to forget about me. Every day since I first entered the Forbidden City, I have lived in fear. Fear of being discovered. Fear of being put to death for deceiving his majesty. I don't know how I ended up here."

I look at Huiyin, waiting for her to say something, anything. Surprisingly, I'm not crying. I don't regret opening up to her. I only feel relief, like a heavy boulder that had been crushing me is lifted from my chest and I can breathe for the first time in over a year.

Huiyin watches me for another long moment. Finally, she takes my hand again. "You ended up here because it is where you are supposed to be," she says.

Now I do let out a small sob. "Do you really think so?"

She nods. "You just saved China from a war. How can you think that you are supposed to be anywhere else?"

I pull her to me in a tight hug. I cry. I let out long, heaving sobs, sobs I have held inside for so long. I cry for my family. I still miss them so much. I miss knowing where they are and what they are doing. I miss knowing if they are safe. I cry for the fear I have felt every single day. I cry for the friends I have made here: Huiyin, Suyin, Yanmei, Jinhai. I cry for my children, Dongmei and Jingfei. I cry for Caihong. I cry for Honghui. Finally, I cry for myself. I don't want to die. As much as I hate to admit it, I love my life. I am happy, I am surrounded by love. I am safe and comfortable.

I cry because I am about to lose everything all over again.

When I was chosen as a concubine, my life with my family, my life as a Han Chinese, was over. It was not much of a life. I was poor with no marriage prospects. But it was my life, the only one I knew. I thought that I would never recover. That I would never find a new place in the world. But I was wrong. I found a new place, a place among the Manchu. Life is not perfect, and I am still conflicted over considering Manchu people my family after all they have done to the people of China. But it is the only life I have. The one I built from nothing. The thought of now losing all I have for the second time is a pain so deep, I think it might be better to die after all.

Huiyin finally pulls away from me. She picks up the cloth and wipes my face. "There, there," she says kindly and with a smile, "it is not right for the empress to weep so."

I chuckle. "You still think I'm an empress?"

"Yes," she says without hesitation. "You are the empress because Heaven wills it. If you die, you should die knowing that you fulfilled your great purpose. And if you don't die, it is because Heaven has a plan for you yet still."

A shiver runs down my spine at her words. I think she must be right. Many times, I have only been able to credit Heaven for my rise to empress. It certainly was not because I wanted it. If Huiyin can see that as well, then it must be true.

I take a few breaths to calm myself. "Thank you," I say. "I have wanted to tell someone that for so long."

"I am honored that you put your trust in me, your majesty," she says. She then turns my face to her again. "Now, can we make you presentable? The general and Prince Honghui will not want to be kept waiting forever."

I nod and let my features relax. I do not know what will happen next, but I will face it with my head held high.

25

———

When my makeup is finally done, Huiyin styles my hair and helps me dress, which is not easy with my arm bandaged the way it is. I try to wear a pair of pot-bottom shoes, but the pain in my hip makes it impossible to balance. I have to settle for a pair of silk slippers, which makes my robe drag along the floor. I'm certain I look more ridiculous than regal, but there's no help for it.

Huiyin then escorts me to the main audience hall. I am terribly nervous, my stomach fluttering and clenching in turn. Prince Honghui is waiting for me, and I have no idea how he is going to react. I expect him to be furious.

I had expected to see General Pake and Prince Honghui in the audience hall, but I am surprised to see well over a hundred men waiting for me. Both foreign men and the emperor's advisors and lords are present, all dressed as if they were waiting to see the emperor himself. There is a table set up at the bottom of the stairs that lead up to the emperor's throne. High above the throne, the massive, golden dragon with the pearl in its mouth hovers. Even though no one is sitting on the throne, I expect the dragon to drop the pearl at any moment, sending it crashing down the stairs and rolling over anyone in its path.

At each end of the table stand General Pake and Prince Honghui. I grip Huiyin's hand as Honghui looks at me, his face dark, his brow furrowed. His eyes go wide when he sees me and then he yells something in English at General Pake. They have a bit of a back and forth.

"The prince is upset and accusing the general of causing you harm," Huiyin explains.

"It's my fault," I say, interrupting the men and speaking directly to Honghui. "No one here has hurt me. Everyone has been very courteous."

Honghui glares at me for a moment before speaking to General Pake again. There is more back and forth before the general motions to the large parchment in the middle of the table. The general addresses the crowd, then he dips a pen into an ink well and signs the paper. Prince Honghui signs as well, but he does not speak before doing so. He practically throws the pen down when he is done, as if it has offended him somehow. And I suppose it has. I have no idea what the terms of the treaty are, or what they might mean for China, except that they are unfair to us. I know Honghui said he would sign to save the country from war, but the terms are still distasteful.

After Honghui signs, the general smiles and claps, and all the foreigners in the crowd clap as well. The general and Prince Honghui shake hands, and the ceremony seems to be complete. The people disperse and the large doors to the front of the audience hall are opened. Prince Honghui motions toward the door to me, and Huiyin helps me walk outside, where a donkey cart is waiting for me. This is not a cheap, open-air donkey cart like what we used to escape the palace when the foreigners invaded, but an imperial one, with a covering and flaps to protect me from the elements and lined with silks and furs.

"What happens next?" I ask Honghui.

"We are to return to the Winter Palace," he says with no warmth in his voice. He is barely even looking at me. "The foreigners have thirty days to leave Peking. Emperor Guozhi refuses to return to the city as long as a single foreigner remains." He pulls a flap back and motions for me to climb into the cart. I am frustrated by his curt manner with, and it frightens me. If he is this angry with me, how much more angry must Guozhi be?

"This is where I leave you," Huiyin says. I feel her start to pull her hand away, but I grip it tighter. I think she must see the fear on my face. She pats my cheek. "Be brave, your majesty. Remember, whatever happens next is what is supposed to happen."

I nod, but I can't speak. My old fears return and I am on the verge of tears again. Huiyin gives me a gentle hug, kisses my cheek, and then returns to the audience hall, turning her back on me, her country, and her people forever.

"Who was that?" Honghui asks me.

I shake my head. "It doesn't matter." I don't see why he needs to know that it is another one of the emperor's women who did what she thought was best instead of what was expected of her. She should have chosen death over infidelity. But she didn't. She chose happiness instead, and I hope she never regrets that choice. Like Wangli, I want nothing but joy for her.

"Come on," he says, a little more gently than before. "We need to go."

"Must we?" I ask, my courage certainly failing me. "Is Guozhi... Will Guozhi... Will he kill me?"

"I don't know, Lihua," he says with a sigh, as if he is ready for this whole affair to be at an end. I have to grit my teeth to keep from telling him to call me Daiyu. If he were to find out right now that I have been lying to him all this time, I cannot predict how he would react. If I want to have any hope of my life being spared, I will need Honghui on my side.

"Guozhi is furious," he finally admits, looking down at me. "He believes you have betrayed your country, your people, and most of all, him."

"I may have gone against his will," I say, "but I did not betray my people. *Our* people. I did it for them. They are the only reason I did this. Guozhi was going to let them die. Let the foreigners slaughter them, raze the fields, let us starve. I protected our people, not Guozhi. Not the emperor. Not the supposed Son of Heaven."

"Lihua!" Honghui growls at me, grabbing my arm. I scream in pain and Honghui releases me. I open my robe and show him my arm in its sling. His face softens. "What happened to you?"

"I was thrown from your horse," I say, pulling my robe around me again. "When the soldiers wouldn't let me into the Forbidden City, I charged them. They shot the horse and I fell to the ground. The doctor said I was lucky to be alive. But my arm will be terribly scarred when it heals."

Honghui is quiet for a moment, then he sighs. "I know why you did this. I understand your motives. I know you thought you were doing the right thing. But Guozhi... To him, there is no excuse for disloyalty. I do not know if he will kill you, but he will not let you go unpunished."

I nod. "I will have to accept whatever decision he makes."

We look at each other for a long, silent moment. I want to ask him to protect me. To save me. And I think he is searching his brain to try and find a way to help me. But I cannot ask such a thing of him. He has already risked so much for me.

"Come on, then," he says. He gently takes my other arm and helps me into the cart. I situate myself on the silk pillows, trying to find a way to sit comfortably, but it is a lost cause. Honghui closes and ties the flap shut, and a moment later, the cart is bouncing along the rough road.

I lay down on my right side and try to sleep, but the cart shakes me like a bag of rice. I think riding the horse was more comfortable, and that was rather terrible. I wouldn't be able to ride a horse in my present condition, though. My leg hurts too badly to hold me in the saddle, and I wouldn't be able to use my left hand to grip the reins.

All I can do for the duration of the long, terrible ride is imagine how my meeting with Guozhi will go. I suppose I will throw myself at his feet. Beg for mercy. Plead ignorance and stupidity. I am just an idiot girl, even after everything. I don't know how any of this will play out. If I actually saved lives or not. If China will be better or worse under the new treaty. I don't suppose I will ever know. I'll either be dead, or I will be once again sequestered behind the tall, red walls of the Forbidden City, unaware of what is going on outside.

Finally, after several days of traveling, the cart slows to a stop. As I wait for someone to open the flap, I begin to hear voices. Many voices. I realize that the crowd of people outside the Winter Palace is still there. I had assumed that they would return home after the treaty was signed, but I suppose they are waiting for the foreigners to actually leave the city, like the emperor is doing.

I wonder if the people have heard what has happened. What I have done. How I betrayed them by giving myself up to the foreign general. I am starting to wish that Honghui had led the cart all the way inside the palace before stopping. I don't want to face a riot.

The flap is opened and Honghui reaches his hand inside for me. I step out into the light and have to blink a few times in order to see. When my vision returns, I see that the guards are holding back the crowd.

"Get back! Stay back!" they order. I stand a little closer to Honghui, but I then realize the people don't appear angry. If anything, they are crying, reaching for me, just like they did when I was bringing them food.

"There she is!" someone says.

"Your Majesty!"

"Empress, help me!"

"What is going on?" I ask Honghui.

He shakes his head. "I don't know. They have been calling for you non-stop since you left."

"What?" I am completely dumbfounded.

One elderly man is on his knees, reaching through the legs of the guards for me. "Empress! Empress!"

I step away from Honghui and kneel down as best I can, taking the man's hand in mine. "What is wrong?"

"Thank you, my lady," he says.

"For what?"

"You saved my son."

"How?"

"He said you ended the war," the man says. "You let all the men who had been recruited into the emperor's army go free."

I shake my head. "No. I did no such thing."

"You did," the man says. "I know you did. We all know that it had to be you who stopped the war. Only you have shown a care for any of us. Thank you." His hand slips from mine and he is quickly lost in the crowd.

"It seems they have heard about what you did," Honghui says. "They credit you with ending the war."

"May the empress live ten-thousand years! May the empress live ten-thousand years!" the crowd chants over and over again. The sound grows louder and louder, echoing off the surrounding mountains.

"But...I forced us to surrender," I tell Honghui. "We didn't win the war."

"They don't understand any of that," Honghui says. "They are simple people. They only know that war, death, and famine were coming. Now, all of that is gone and they will soon be able to return to their homes. They thank you for that."

I shake my head in disbelief. I don't know how the people can know what happened between two great powers on the brink of war. What do they know of taxes and treaties? But I suppose they don't need to. For them, it is very simple. They saw me riding a horse to Peking, and then the war came to an end. I watch as the entire crowd of people drops to their knees and kowtows to me.

"May the empress live ten-thousand years! May the empress live ten-thousand years!"

I shake my head and put my hand to my mouth to hide a small smile. It might seem strange. After all, I betrayed the emperor. He might order my death. My life may be at an end very soon. But right now, for just a moment, it feels good to know that at least a few people know that I did everything I could to save them. That I *did* save them. That I was willing to risk my life to avert a war.

I think that Huiyin was right. I can face whatever comes next because I finally did something great with my life. I didn't just save Lihua from being trapped in the harem. I didn't just save my family from poverty. I saved lives. So many lives. More than I can count.

What is one life when compared with so many others?

26

Prince Honghui leads me to the emperor's bed-chamber. When I step into the room, I gag and have to put my finger to my nose, the smell is so pungent. I see the doctor and several eunuchs around the emperor's bed. When they see me, they stop what they are doing and bow, giving me a view of the emperor.

"What's happened to you?" I ask, rushing to his side. His face looks almost green, he is so ill. He grimaces, in obvious pain.

"Get back, witch," he says, slapping at my hand as I reach for him, but the attempt is weak. "Leave us!" he hisses to everyone else. The doctor and eunuchs back out of the room quickly, but Honghui lingers. I can't believe he didn't tell me that Guozhi's health had decayed so rapidly. I had imagined that he would be nearly back to full health upon my return. As it is, I'm surprised he's still alive.

"Out!" Guozhi says to Honghui, his voice raw. Honghui hesitates, but then he backs out of the room, closing the door behind him.

"How could you, Lihua?" he asks with a cough. "How could you betray me like that?"

I get on my knees. "I am sorry. I was afraid. I was afraid for you, for me, for everyone. I thought that if you did not sign the treaty, then we would all die—"

"That was my choice!" he says, pounding his fist on the bedcovers. "My right as emperor. It is not up to you to challenge my decisions. If I want every person in this kingdom to sacrifice their life, then they must obey! My word is law!"

My voice fails me. He is being completely unreasonable. I have to wonder if the sickness has infected his brain. I realize that nothing I say can help the situation.

"Yes, your majesty," I say. "I beg for your mercy."

"Mercy?" he says, then he coughs again. "I should have you dragged from this room and beaten to death."

I tremble with terror, but I nod. "I know." My voice cracks and tears pool in my eyes.

"That was my plan," he says, his voice a little calmer. "As soon as I heard what you did, I branded you a traitor and was going to have you executed as soon as you were returned."

"I knew the risk I was taking," I say.

He shakes his head in disbelief. "Then, why? If you knew that your actions would merit death, why would you do it?"

"You might be the emperor, but you are still only one man. My thoughts were with the hundreds of people outside who were depending on you to protect them. The thousands, millions of people in China who might die if the war continued. My life is insignificant in comparison."

"Do you know what you have done?" Guozhi asks me. "Do you know the terms of the treaty my brother signed?"

"No."

"Of course you don't," he says. "You are just a stupid, ignorant girl."

"Yes."

"You have meddled in affairs you cannot possibly understand."

I stay quiet because he is right.

"You think you saved lives, but you may very well have cost lives as well."

His words frighten me. "What do you mean?"

"The treaty laid all the blame for the conflict at my feet," he says. "Because of that, I must now pay thousands of taels of gold in penalty. Do you know where that money will come from?"

I shake my head.

"Taxes, Lihua. That money comes from the people you were so desperate to protect. People who you yourself have said many times are already impoverished."

My heart beats rapidly in my chest. I can't imagine the already overtaxed people being able to pay even more money to the government.

"I had to agree to a lower tax rate on foreign imports and exports, so that is even more money lost. I had to end the ban on importing opium. Opium is a vile substance. Foolish, weak-minded people will eat opium instead of food until they starve. Until their families starve."

I had known opium-eaters when I lived in the hutongs. They would sacrifice everything for a little bit of black tar in their pipe until they had nothing left. And when they could no longer pay, the opium den owners would throw them out into the street until they starved or froze to death.

"I had to give them land, whole islands! A province in the north. Even land within Peking itself where the foreigners can do whatever they want and pay no heed to our laws."

I wipe my leaking nose and the tears from my cheeks. I had no idea. I knew the terms were harsh, but I still thought that they must be better than open warfare. And Prince Honghui said he would sign the treaty. But I suppose that could have been an earlier version of the terms. Once the foreigners had me in custody, they could make any demands they wanted. The fact that I might have made things even worse for the people makes me sick.

I move back away from the bed and do a full kowtow with my forehead to the floor, paying no heed to the pain in my body. "I'm sorry. I'm so sorry. I didn't know."

"I believe your heart was in the right place, Lihua," the emperor says, not unkindly. "I have never known you to act out of malice. But your actions are unforgivable."

I cry, my face still to the floor, as I wait for him to pass his sentence. I only hope I will have the strength to bear it.

"You are no longer my empress," he says. "Neither are you my consort or concubine. Your existence in the palace records will be completely destroyed. It will be as if you never lived."

I groan in despair. Everything I have ever done has been in the service of others. I have completely given up my life twice. But now, even my very existence will disappear with my death. My sacrifices will be lost and I will be forgotten.

"It is only out of my love for Caihong that I do not have your head removed from your body," the emperor says. It takes me a long moment to understand his words since they are not what I expected to hear.

"Wha-what?" I finally say.

"You saved Caihong's life from the assassin," he says.

"The fact that she died later was not your fault. You saved Caihong's life, and now I have spared yours."

"Thank you!" I cry, knocking my forehead to the floor again. I'm not going to die! I can hardly believe it. "Your majesty is truly kind and gracious!"

"You will be taken to the Temple of Grief, where you still live the rest of your days as a nun. Your life will be as that of a widow."

I had heard of the Temple of Grief, but I have never been there. It is an abbey situated on a mountain north of Peking. Whenever an emperor dies, his surviving consorts and concubines—except for the empress dowager—are sent there to live out their days. No matter how young the widows may be, they are not allowed to remarry and are expected to live the rest of the lives in mourning for their dead emperor. Considering that most consorts and concubines never had children of their own, it is not a happy end to their lives. Very few can ever claim to have had a real marriage to their emperor, and they are forbidden from ever having one with someone else. It is called the Temple of Grief because the women are expected to spend their lives grieving for the emperor. But I had always thought it was called that because the women are grieving for themselves. Perhaps it is both.

"Are you not grateful?" the emperor asks me, his breathing becoming labored.

"Yes," I say. "Of course! I am only in shock at his majesty's great mercy toward me." I had been thinking about what life at a temple would mean for me and hadn't thanked him for sparing my life. "You are truly kind and merciful and I am not worthy of the generosity you have shown to me."

"Leave me," he says, closing his eyes. "I am tired and do

not wish to see your face again. You will be taken to the abbey immediately. Your life here is finished."

I get to my feet, my knees weak and my hip sore, but I do not complain as I back out of the room, thanking him with every step. He closes his eyes and sleeps before I am out the door.

In the courtyard, Fiyanggu is speaking to Honghui. Honghui is chewing on his thumb and nodding. When he sees me, he looks up, and I see relief on his face. He walks over to me and I am so relieved and weak I must lean on his arm for assistance.

"Fiyanggu has told me what your sentence is," Honghui says when I reach him. "You are quite fortunate."

"I know," I say. "I am so grateful."

"Come," Honghui says. "I will escort you to the temple."

"Please," I say, tugging on his arm, "may I say goodbye to my friends, my servants? To Dongmei and Jingfei?" Honghui hesitates and looks to Fiyanggu. Fiyanggu gives a small nod and then backs away out of the courtyard.

"Fine," Honghui says. "But you must be quick about it. You should not linger lest my brother change his mind."

"He told me about the terms of the treaty," I say as we leave the emperor's courtyard. "I feel like such a fool. I had meant to save China, save my people, but I have only condemned them to a much worse life."

"Guozhi exaggerates," Honghui says. "The treaty is absurd, yes. But I agree with you that war would be worse. Treaties can always be renegotiated. But the damage done in war cannot be undone."

I let out a sigh of relief. "So, you are not angry with me? You think I did the right thing?"

He is quiet for a moment, looking at me with his deep, dark eyes. He shakes his head and shrugs. "Who can say?

What is done is done. You are alive, and the war is at an end. I could not have hoped for a better outcome."

Relief washes over me and I feel a little lightheaded. Honghui places his hand on my back to steady me, then he cups my cheek, rubbing the side of my face with his thumb. His hand drops when we hear voices approaching.

Dongmei and Jingfei run toward me. I drop down and hold them in my arms. "My darlings," I say. My heart breaks to leave them. They will once again be motherless. That will be my biggest regret for the rest of my life, I believe.

"Must you leave?" Dongmei asks.

"Please stay!" Jingfei cries.

"I am sorry," I say. "But I must go. It is your father's will."

"Can we visit you?" Dongmei asks.

I do not know the answer, but I nod. I cannot leave them without some hope. "Someday." I hug them again, kissing them on their cheeks. I stand and hug Yanmei.

"Take care of them," I tell her, "and of yourself."

"I will," she says. "I will miss you so much."

"And I you," I say, squeezing her hands. I then turn to my faithful servants, Suyin and Jinhai. I hug each of them in turn, thanking them for taking such good care of me.

"I will come with you," Suyin says.

I shake my head. "No, you cannot. You should leave this place. Don't ask for a reassignment. You have plenty of money saved. You must leave here and return to your family. Use the money as a dowry. Marry and have lots of children. I'll not let your life come to an end for me."

Her eyes water and she nods. I give her another hug. Suyin holds me so tightly, I can't let go of her, and she nods. "I will do as you say, your majesty." I smile and pat her cheek.

I then turn to Jinhai. His gentle face is streaked with

tears. I pull him to me and whisper in his ear. "You and Suyin know where the money and jewels are hidden. Divide them among you and then go live happy lives far away from this place."

He nods, crying so hard he cannot speak. I back away, taking one long last look at the people who have become my family. To leave my family a second time hurts more than I can put into words.

A eunuch announces that the empress dowager has approached. Everyone turns to face her and kneels, even me. I am no longer the empress, so I must bow before her once again. There is a satisfied smile on her face as she approaches me, Euhmeh by her side.

"I told you that you would not be empress for long," Fenfeng says. "Though, I never imagined you would sabotage yourself so spectacularly."

I rise to my feet and stand before her, my chin held high. "I sacrificed everything for the people of this country. Could you ever say the same?"

Everyone gasps and the smile falls from Fenfeng's face. She steps even closer to me until we are nearly chest to chest.

"How dare you, you insolent little bug," she hisses.

"Insult me all you want, Mother," I say. "You can't hurt me anymore."

As heartbroken as I am to be leaving, I suppose there is one advantage to no longer being empress—I am no longer under the thumb of the empress dowager.

I expect her rage to grow. For her to scream and stomp her feet. But she doesn't. Instead, she chuckles as she bends close to my ear and whispers so that only I can hear her.

"Caihong once thought that too," she says.

Her words nearly knock me off balance as my mind whirls. "What...what did you do to Caihong?"

"Thanks to you, nothing," Fenfeng says. "If only poor Lady An hadn't gotten the blame, everything would have been set to right. But you had to get in the way, didn't you?"

Panic grips my chest. Lady An? Caihong? The assassin! Fenfeng was the one behind it all? I don't understand. I look around, hoping that someone else is hearing what she's saying, but there is no one in earshot.

"Why?" I ask her, so confused.

"It doesn't matter now," she says as she reaches up and dusts something invisible from my shoulder. "I'm only glad I lived long enough to see this. And don't worry about his majesty. He will find comfort in someone far more worthy." She looks over at Euhmeh, a smirk on her face.

I'm nearly sick with rage, but there is nothing I can do! I can't accuse the emperor's mother of such a heinous crime without evidence. She tried to kill Caihong! Lady An died because of her. And she's gotten away with it all.

I take a step back from her, eager to get away. Away from her. Away from this place. Away from such malice and hatred and betrayal. There is a stabbing sensation in my stomach and I turn to Honghui. I give him a nod and he leads me out of the Winter Palace for the last time.

"What did she say?" he asks me.

I shake my head. "It doesn't matter now." I hardly comprehend what Fenfeng has done, what her words truly mean. I can only hope that one day I will be able to sort them out and somehow get justice for Caihong and Lady An.

There is still a crowd of people outside, and when they see me, they cheer.

"May the empress live ten-thousand years! May the empress live ten-thousand years!"

"Someone will have to tell them that I am no longer the empress," I mutter to Honghui.

"Not today," he says. He opens the flap to the donkey cart and I climb back inside.

The cart rocks this way and that as it lumbers down an eastern path away from the Winter Palace and the cheering slowly fades into the distance.

27

We travel for several days at a sedate pace. The evenings are quiet as Honghui and I and the two guards who accompanied us sit around the fire. There is so much unsaid between myself and Honghui, but we are not alone. I wrestle in my mind with telling him the truth of my existence. I want to tell him. I long to tell him. But if this is the last time I will ever see him, I do not want him to leave thinking ill of me. Thinking me a liar and deceiver.

We travel far to the north and east, up into the mountains where leafy trees turn to spruce and the ground is littered with brown pine needles. The smell is divine for trees so ugly.

The villages we pass and quiet and peaceful. The war seems not to have touched this area at all. I imagine most of the country has no idea how close we came to war. "Heaven is high above and the emperor is far away," so they say. Do these people even know who the emperor is? They certainly take no notice of us as we pass through except to sell us food.

The road becomes more rough the farther we travel, the

ruts deep, jostling me around. I fear my teeth will be shaken right out of my head. I am so thankful when we finally stop. I poke my head out of the cart, expecting to see the abbey, but there is nothing around us except trees.

"Why have we stopped?" I ask.

"We will have to take the horse from here," Honghui says. One of the guards helps me out of the cart and I see that the road is so uneven and covered with stones the donkey could not hope to pull the cart any further.

"Looks like there have been heavy rains recently, making the road impassable," Honghui explains.

I nod, but I am nervous about spending time alone with Honghui. He offers me his hand and pulls me up onto the horse so that I sit sideways in front of him. In my condition, I could not hope to sit on a saddle properly.

"Head back," Honghui tells the guards. "I will catch back up with you soon." The guards nod and turn the cart about, heading back down the mountain.

Honghui urges his horse up the path, but it is slow going. The horse must step carefully to avoid tripping in the ruts or on errant stones. Riding on the horse is barely more comfortable than riding in the cart. I wrap my arms around Honghui's waist to keep from falling off and lean my head into his chest.

"You are lucky," Honghui finally says. "I truly thought Guozhi was going to order your death."

"So did I," I say. "I was prepared to face death."

Honghui seems surprised to hear me say this. "I wasn't prepared for you to die."

"Could you have stopped it?"

"I am glad it didn't come to that," he says. "If I'd had to choose between you or my brother...I don't know who would have won out."

I am glad that Honghui didn't have to make that choice. Equally am I glad that I didn't have to face the executioner. I like to think that I would have been strong. Brave. But who can know until the moment of death arrives?

Honghui's body tenses and he brings the horse to a stop. "I don't have to take you to the abbey."

I sit up. "What?"

He turns around in the saddle to face me. "I could take you somewhere else. Or just leave you here and you could find your way to the nearest village."

My mouth gapes. I look back down the road and see that the guards and donkey cart are long gone. He's right. I could get off this horse and run away into the woods and then go...anywhere.

But where would I go?

I don't know where I am. And I don't know where my parents are. I don't have any money or extra clothes or food. I'm sure Honghui could give me some money, but that would run out eventually. I don't particularly want to live in a nunnery. But for now, at least, I will have somewhere to sleep and food to eat.

I shake my head. "I don't have anywhere to go."

He looks confused and thinks about this for a moment. "What about your mother? Aren't you the daughter of a general?"

I look at him for a long time. Long enough for him to realize the truth, at least partly. He doesn't ask for more information, and the words are stuck in my chest. I open my mouth, but nothing comes out. Honghui pulls my head to his chest as he urges the horse to continue.

"Will Guozhi die?" I ask. He looked so ill, so weak, it makes me wonder how he is even still alive. Will he be dead by the time Honghui returns?

"I don't know," Honghui says. "The doctor says that he could die, but also that there is an equal chance he will live. Pray for him when you reach the abbey."

"I will," I say. Guozhi spared my life. I hope the gods will be equally merciful with him.

Finally, we came to the end of the road where stone steps led even further up the mountain. A stone, arched gateway stands sentinel at the bottom of the stairs. At the top of the arch is carved the characters for Temple of Grief, and blessings are etched down on each side. The archway is ornately engraved and painted in red and blue and yellow. It is not bland or stoic, as I expected a nunnery to be, but quite beautiful. Honghui climbs off the horse and then helps me slide down in front of him. He doesn't let me go.

"This is where I leave you," Honghui says and I feel a sudden pang in my heart.

I reach up and put my hand behind his neck. "Will I ever see you again?" I ask.

He cups my cheek. "I can only hope so. Men are not allowed inside the temple, but who knows where fate will lead us."

I nod and sniff to keep from crying. He places his lips on mine, gently. The sensation is bittersweet. Joy mixed with tears.

"I love you," he says. I can't hold back the tears and bury my face in his chest.

"It's not fair," I say. "It's not fair!"

"I know," he says, rocking me. "But you are alive. That is the most important thing. This is not the end. Not the end of you; not the end of us. We will find our way back to each other, I am certain."

We kiss again and hold each other tight. The longer I

tarry, the harder it becomes to leave him. I let my arm slip from his shoulder and take a step back.

His eyes are red, but he refuses to cry. Instead, he bows.

"Farewell, empress."

"I'm not the empress anymore," I say.

"You will always be my empress."

My heart feels as though it is being stabbed with a hundred needles, but I keep my feet firmly on the ground. If I go to him again, I'll never let him go.

Honghui climbs up onto his horse and turns it away from me, walking back down the dangerous, rocky path. I watch as he disappears down the trail. He never looks back. I don't think he can.

As soon as he is out of sight, I turn back to the long, winding staircase. I am surprised to see a woman coming down the stairs. She is older, her head is shaved, and she is wearing a loose-fitting, orange robe. I go up the stairs, through the archway, and meet her halfway. She has a smile on her face, and her cheeks are full and rosy. She seems happy and healthy. I suppose I had expected the women here to be miserable, starving creatures.

"Greetings, little sister," she says with a bow. "What brings you here?"

"I was ordered to come here," I say. "I was one of Emperor Guozhi's consorts."

The woman gasps, putting her hands to her mouth. "Has the emperor died?"

"No," I say, putting my hand on her arm reassuringly. "No, the emperor is not dead."

"Then why are you... Oh, I see." She nods. "You are not the first concubine to be sent to us in disgrace."

"I wasn't a concubine," I say. "Well, I started out as one. But before I was sent here, I was the empress."

The woman raises an eyebrow. "This is a story I am looking forward to hearing."

"I'd love to be able to tell you everything, if it is safe to do so," I hedge.

The woman chuckles and wraps an arm around my shoulders. "You are quite young. You are going to be here a *very* long time. I am sure you will learn to trust me in time."

Her kind and warm demeanor sets me at ease. Coming here might have been the best thing for me after all. I feel almost guilty that the emperor sent me here as a punishment. It feels more like a reward.

We take a few more steps up the stairs and the abbey starts to come into view. It looks almost like a palace. The building is gray, but the roof is ornately curled and painted bright colors. At the top of the stairs, a large courtyard sits within half a dozen buildings. In the middle of the courtyard stands a covered incense hearth from which smoke from smoldering joss sticks floats up into the sky. The courtyard is an exquisite garden with flowers of every color. There are ponds and rookeries and places to sit and meditate. Small cats and dogs run around playfully, along with a few chickens.

But what is most amazing is that there are also dozens of women. They are all older than me, but some not by much. They all have shaved heads and wear matching orange robes. They are tending the flowers, painting, doing embroidery, all the usual feminine pastimes. But they are all so happy! They are chatting and laughing, working together, with genuine smiles on their faces.

From somewhere, a gong is struck, and at once, all the women stop what they are doing and walk to the back of the courtyard to a large building with a wide-open front. I can see several women kneeling and kowtowing to something deeper in the shadows of the building. An altar of some sort, I assume.

"I am the senior teacher here," the woman I am with says. "You may call me Tao Fashi. What should I call you?"

"Daiyu," I say without hesitation. "My name is Daiyu."

Daiyu's adventure continues in Empress in Danger,
available for pre-order now at your favorite bookstore!
https://books2read.com/u/49l78k

Be sure to sign up for our mailing lists so you never miss a
new release!
http://zoeygong.com/subscribe/
http://amandarobertswrites.com/empress-in-disguise/

EMPRESS IN DANGER
EMPRESS IN DISGUISE BOOK 3

https://books2read.com/u/49l78k

She thought that fate was finished with her. But it was only beginning…

After being banished to a remote abbey, Daiyu thinks the machinations of the inner court can no longer hurt her. But she is wrong. A ghost from the past emerges and threatens everything Daiyu has worked so hard to build for herself.

From the opulence of the inner court and the right hand of the emperor, Daiyu finds herself back at the beginning, back outside the imposing red walls of the Forbidden City. Daiyu discovers that she has the power to choose her future, but both futures carry a risk she is not sure she has the strength to face.

But underneath it all is a love so powerful, Daiyu cannot walk away.

The future of the Chinese empire rests with her...

ABOUT ZOEY GONG

ZOEY GONG was born and raised in rural Hunan Province, China. She has been studying English and working as a translator since she was sixteen years old. Now in her early twenties, Zoey loves traveling and eating noodles for every meal. She lives in Shenzhen with her cat, Jello, and dreams of one day disappointing her parents by being a Leftover Woman (剩女). Learn more at ZoeyGong.com.

facebook.com/ZoeyGongAuthor

goodreads.com/zoeygong

bookbub.com/authors/zoey-gong

ABOUT AMANDA ROBERTS

 Amanda Roberts is a USA Today best-selling author who has been living in China since 2010. She has an MA in English from the University of Central Missouri and has been published in magazines, newspapers, and anthologies around the world. Amanda can be found all over the Internet, but her home is AmandaRobertsWrites.com.

facebook.com/AmandaRobertsWrites

instagram.com/amandarobertswrites

goodreads.com/Amanda_Roberts

bookbub.com/authors/amanda-roberts-2bfe99dd-ea16-4614-a696-84116326dcd1

ABOUT THE PUBLISHER

RED EMPRESS PUBLISHING

Visit Our Website To See All Of Our Diverse Books
http://www.redempresspublishing.com

Quality trade paperbacks, downloads, audio books, and books in foreign languages in genres such as historical, romance, mystery, and fantasy.